CW01190294

Attack of the Sea Devil

Around Halberd the crew screamed his name as they raced to the port side, swords drawn and arrows nocked. Rising high above the swells was the serpent of his dreams. Green and showering sea water from its scales, the demon uncoiled and peered down at the ship. Its eyes were flame, pure flame. Its fangs were longer than the mast and almost as broad.

Halberd drew his sword and called to his crew. "It is an apparition! Do not waste your arrows!"

At the sound of his voice, the serpent turned its giant head and spotted Halberd. Instantly it struck. Its great tooth caught his arm and, dragging along its length, drew a gout of blood. As Halberd fell back on the deck, clutching his wounded arm, he could plainly see, in the eyes of the demon, the laughing face of Grettir. . . .

SIGNET SCIENCE FICTION

WHERE NO MAN HAS GONE BEFORE . . .

(0451)

☐ **GOLDEN WITCHBREED by Mary Gentle.** Earth envoy Lynne Christie has been sent to Orthe to establish contact and determine whether this is a world worth developing. But suddenly Christie finds herself a hunted fugitive on an alien world and her only chance of survival lies in saving Orthe itself from a menace older than time (136063—$3.95)†

☐ **DRIFTGLASS by Samuel R. Delany.** From Ganymede to Gomorrah, a bizarre breed of planet-hopping humans sell their sexless, neutered bodies . . . so that others may explore the outer limits of sexual perversion Delany's universe is rooted in the present, projected into the future. It is an existence where anything can happen—and does! (144244—$2.95)*

☐ **THE WIND FROM THE SUN by Arthur C. Clarke.** Can anyone journey farther than Arthur C. Clarke, through the universe? Board the Clarke starship to the future and experience his eighteen wonders of the imagination for yourself! "Highly recommended."—*Library Journal* (147545—$3.50)*

☐ **EMILE AND THE DUTCHMAN by Joel Rosenberg.** Their mission was simple—the survival of the human race. It should have been no problem for the two toughest, cleverest mavericks in outer space . . . that is until they found themselves pitted against the most cunning and deadly of intergalactic aliens (140168—$2.95)

*Prices slightly higher in Canada
†Not available in Canada

Buy them at your local bookstore or use this convenient coupon for ordering.

NEW AMERICAN LIBRARY,
P.O. Box 999, Bergenfield, New Jersey 07621

Please send me the books I have checked above. I am enclosing $________ (please add $1.00 to this order to cover postage and handling). Send check or money order—no cash or C.O.D.'s. Prices and numbers subject to change without notice.

Name ________________________________

Address ________________________________

City______________State____________Zip Code__________

Allow 4-6 weeks for delivery.
This offer is subject to withdrawal without notice.

HALBERD, DREAM WARRIOR

LLOYD ST. ALCORN

A SIGNET BOOK

NEW AMERICAN LIBRARY

NAL BOOKS ARE AVAILABLE AT QUANTITY DISCOUNTS WHEN USED TO PROMOTE PRODUCTS OR SERVICES. FOR INFORMATION PLEASE WRITE TO PREMIUM MARKETING DIVISION, NEW AMERICAN LIBRARY, 1633 BROADWAY, NEW YORK, NEW YORK 10019.

Copyright © 1987 by David N. Meyer II

All rights reserved

SIGNET TRADEMARK REG. U.S. PAT. OFF. AND FOREIGN COUNTRIES
REGISTERED TRADEMARK—MARCA REGISTRADA
HECHO EN CHICAGO, U.S.A.

SIGNET, SIGNET CLASSIC, MENTOR, ONYX, PLUME, MERIDIAN and NAL BOOKS are published by NAL PENGUIN INC., 1633 Broadway, New York, New York 10019

First Printing, October, 1987

1 2 3 4 5 6 7 8 9

PRINTED IN THE UNITED STATES OF AMERICA

To
Evan & John
and
John & Evan

Prologue

AND HALBERD DREAMED:

Smooth black rocks stretched to the edge of the sea. The water lapped gently at the stones, hissing in between. No waves crashed on the ghostly shore. There was no beach, no birds, no breeze, no sound. Thick gray clouds hung close overhead. It was cold.

Strange clouds appeared on the horizon, moving across the surface of the leaden sea. A thick, white fog unrolled, covering everything. Never rising, never falling, the fog reached out until it obliterated the shoreline. When everything was gray it stopped. No wind spurred it, no wind stirred it. The gray world waited.

A ruined hand reached out of the fog. It was gashed and broken and blood ran from under the fingernails. A bloody head followed. The hand became a finger pointing, the head slowly raised to stare into Halberd's face.

It was his brother, Valdane.

He lay flat on his stomach, with only his head upraised. His long hair was matted with blood. His beard was full of gore. His leather jerkin was slashed to ribbons. Blood leaked in slow rivulets from his eyeballs, cutting bright red tear tracks through the black mud on his cheeks. An arrow protruded from his back. His broadsword lay next to him on the black rocks, broken in half. His helmet rocked crazily on the ground, a huge gouge chopped from the noseguard. Blood ran from under his fingernails.

Valdane rose to his knees, gasping from pain, hunching up like an insect. His legs would not answer him. Only his head and arms could move. He had lost a fearsome battle.

He locked his eyes onto Halberd and slowly, painfully, mouthed two words. When Halberd looked into his brother's mouth he could see no tongue. Only a bloody stump remained.

His message delivered, Valdane lowered his head and waited, his bleeding arm and finger raised above his sagging shoulders, pointing at Halberd's heart. Tiny red drops marched down Valdane's arms and vanished into the fog that clung to him like a cape.

Halberd could only stare. He could not move. His thick, muscled arms were paralyzed. His great fighting ax hung in its holster, untouched. His evil stabbing dirk, with its fiendish three sides and blood gutters, lay under his armor, across his back in its hidden scabbard. His broadsword rested against his tent pole. Halberd could reach for none of them.

The ground mist obscuring the beach on which his brother lay began to swirl. A demon was moving along the wet black rocks. Despite his paralysis Halberd was unafraid. He was no stranger to the world of spirits.

The mist bulged upward and formed a pillar. The pillar whirled like a top and became a human form. Yellow-haired and wild-eyed, a witch emerged from the mist. Her breasts heaved beneath her blood-soaked blouse. Her nipples distended the fabric. Though her clothing was soaked, she had suffered no wounds. In her right hand she clutched a strange elongated pyramid of gray stone, a narrow obelisk.

Halberd stared into the mad, beautiful face. Madness and strength, sorcery and evil, glowed in her eyes. There was no human pity, nor anger. There was only feral, animal triumph.

This was no anonymous demon. Halberd knew her well. She was the only woman he had ever loved, the only thing he had desired and not gained. She was Grettir, the wife of his dying brother.

But this was not the Grettir that Halberd had last seen sailing off with Valdane less than a year before. Her lovely blond hair did not hang, free about her shoulders, but was woven around her head in a sorceress' braid. Her long flowing dress was replaced by the thick fur leggings of a warrior and a witch's thin, now blood-drenched, white flaxen shirt. She stood erect and placed her hands on her hips. As she stared at Halberd the mist wrapped around her legs like a contented cat. As always, even as she had at her wedding, Grettir looked at Halberd from the corner of her eyes, as if to say, "If you want me, come and take me. If you conquer me, I will be yours."

She stepped over his brother and straddled

him. Valdane did not turn his head or lower his arm. The blood ran slowly down his fingernails and pooled on his back, dripping and disappearing over his shoulder. The mist covered his lower legs. Grettir dropped into the mist, onto his back with her knees on either side of his once-powerful body. She raised her odd, vicious knife. The elongated pyramid of stone had no handle nor crossguard. The tiny obelisk was thick and sturdy.

Holding the stone knife above her head, Grettir spoke to Halberd in a husky whisper.

"Mark well what I do today, for it is our curse that made me what I am."

Grettir clutched the stone pyramid in both hands. With a battle-scream stolen from the Night Spirits of the northernmost shores she plunged the crude instrument into Valdane's back, cracking his spine and pinning him to the rocky beach. He made no sound as his spine snapped, but the blood gushed from his eyes in a river and poured out of his open mouth.

Grettir wrenched the stone knife from Valdane's back. His body humped slightly upward as she yanked it out. Holding the hollowed-out top of the obelisk to Valdane's wound, she filled the knife with his blood. From her belt Grettir pulled a horn filled with wine. The wine she splashed into the blood. Holding the knife before her in a mocking toast to Halberd, she drank deeply. The gore ran down her chin.

Again she knelt over Valdane and again she drove the gray obelisk into his back. Looking up from the fog that gripped her knees, she laughed. The knife stayed upright in Valdane's back. Again she held Halberd captive with her yellow, cat-like eyes.

"Follow me for your vengeance," she whispered. "Chase me and subdue the curse, chase me and avenge your brother. But beware, Halberd, for the Skrælings have taught me well, and I fear no man. I have power over you, young shaman, power you know nothing of.

"Behold!" cried Grettir, mad beyond fear. She waved a blood-soaked arm behind her, and the mists parted on command. Grettir beckoned to Halberd seductively and pointed a slim finger beyond her shoulder. She was pointing over vast oceans, but on the distant horizon Halberd could see a dim, tree-lined shore, wet and eerie. The trees formed a thick wall, like no shoreline he had ever seen. The trees swung gently in some invisible breeze, welcoming, but at the same time chilling the blood.

"Do you know where that is, little brother?" Grettir purred. "That is the Unknown World, my world, and the Unknown World is where you will find your revenge. Chase me, if you have more courage than your wretched brother! Come to me, my one true love, come to me and die."

Grettir rose to her feet majestically. She stood over her dead husband, her fur-wrapped feet sopping up his blood. She closed her arms to her chest and the mists surrounded her. She vanished. Only his brother's head protruded from the cloaking fog. His thick hair was slowly turning red as the puddle of blood grew ever wider.

The fog receded. The black rocks remained, smooth and dripping wet. His brother lay hunched and broken on the rocks, the stone knife in his back, his blood mingling with the sea as it splashed between the stones.

Halberd thought of his brother's bloody pointing finger and his final unvoiced words. Though strained through bloody teeth, Valdane's message had been clear.

"Avenge me," he had said.

The dream ended.

Halberd awoke.

BOOK ONE

The Wall of Sleep

The Short Ugly People Who Fornicate with Bears

Halberd knew the dream was true. As the icy wind pounded the walls of his house and the snow piled above the door, Halberd lay drenched in sweat. As he fought to reenter the Waking World, the image of Valdane, proud and fearless in the bow of his ship, filled Halberd's mind.

So far as he knew, his brother was thousands of miles across the Northern Sea and the Open Ocean, on the Isle of Vinland, establishing a western camp with his wife and a small troop of his bravest warriors. In the spring Halberd was to sail west and relieve this troop. Spring was three long, stormy months away, and no sane man would venture into the ferocious sea before it arrived. The sea-gods were angriest during the winter and the Giants of the Open Ocean were hungry.

No man had sailed to Vinland before Valdane. No one in their village even knew for certain that Valdane had arrived, but Halberd trusted his dreams to warn him of any harm which might befall his brother.

Now his dreams had spoken.

He knew, with a certainty, that Valdane, his beloved eldest brother, was dead.

Halberd hardly needed the confirmation, but he could not resist a glance at the Jewel of Kyrwyn-Coyne. The jewel glowed, giving off soft rays of amber light into the nighttime, wintertime blackness of the stone house. A few red embers burned beneath the cookpot on the hearth, but the light from the Jewel of Kyrwyn-Coyne was like a small, soft sun.

The mottled amber globe, not quite crystal yet not quite opaque, was a bit smaller than a hen's egg. It rested in a delicate-looking spiderweb of silver filigree attached to the butt of his broadsword handle. The sword rested in its worn leather scabbard.

The Jewel of Kyrwyn-Coyne, proof of Halberd's emerging power as a shaman, glowed only when a dream prophecy was true. Its light broke the darkness only when Halberd left the Waking World and entered the Dream Universe. And now, after the dream which heralded the death of Halberd's brother and proclaimed Grettir a Skræling sorceress, the Jewel gleamed as never before.

His brother dead, his one great love a witch—there was much to think of, but Halberd would not gain strength by dwelling on tragedy. He must deal with his brother's death and formulate his response to Grettir's challenge, but only from a position of strength. And for that strength, he must gain courage from memories of stronger times.

Halberd knew he should avoid the crippling grief that awaited him. Valdane's death demanded action, and action demanded courage. Yet courage demanded confidence. Grief destroyed confidence, daring rebuilt it.

And so Halberd thought of how he had stolen the Jewel of Kyrwyn-Coyne from the Short Ugly People Who Fornicate with Bears.

The Short Ugly People Who Fornicate with Bears lived in the Iron Mountains, in the least accessible portion of the Great Forest which made up the Known Continent. Well to the east of the snow-covered, tree-lined mountains and bays which belong to the Men of the North, the Short Ugly People Who Fornicate with Bears inhabited a few rocky caves and bone-strewn clearings in the foothills of the Iron Mountains, gray barren rocks whose tops streamed with cloud-flags night and day, winter and summer.

The Short Ugly People were the survivors of a long-dead primitive tribe. They were the most savage people in the Known Continent and had been for hundreds of years. No one visited them. No one sought them out for treaties. No one hunted in their lands. Everyone feared them, even the Northmen. Halberd's father, Danyeel, feared them, and he feared nothing.

Men who would step to the battlements of their fortified villages and nock an arrow into a bow against a Northman raiding party would meekly open their gates and offer the Short Ugly People whatever they wanted. No one deliberately sought a battle.

The Short Ugly People Who Fornicate with Bears had low protruding foreheads, black bushy hair, and ugly pushed-in faces. Their arms were knotty and strong, their legs lumpy and powerful. Because their numbers were so few, they mated within their own families. As a result, many had twisted limbs and humped backs. Their language was incomprehensible to outsiders in a continent where every twenty leagues produced a new tongue. Civilized people who tried could communicate well enough.

Every tribe on the Known Continent called them the Short Ugly People Who Fornicate with Bears. They did not refer to themselves by that name, of course. In their own language their tribal name meant "Those Who Are Beloved of God."

People feared the Short Ugly People for good reason. Every Clan's storytelling Great-Great-Great-Grandfather remembered when the vast armies of Short-Sword Men from far to the south came marching up their stone roads in endless rectangular formations. They laid waste to every city and town and subjugated even the Northmen. They could not, however, conquer the Short Ugly People Who Fornicate with Bears.

The Short Ugly People used their mountain caves to good advantage, as well as their poison arrows. They perfected a shaman's poison so strong that a nick from one arrow would send a man into screaming, tormented convulsions. It was widely held that the only death in the Known Continent worse than their poison was to be taken alive by their women, the master torturers of the Great Forest.

Further fear was generated by their gods, the angriest gods in the World. These gods desired death in battle. While every religion saluted heroism and every Northman believed a warrior's death meant a valiant afterlife in Aasgard, no Northman actually preferred death to life. But the lives of the Short Ugly People Who Fornicate with Bears were so mean that their warriors sought death in every fight, no matter how trivial.

No wise man fights a savage armed with poison who desires his own death. So the civilized people left these barbarians alone. And there was yet another, even stronger reason to fear these madmen.

Every spring when the great snows began to melt and the wildlife emerged from its caves ready for the rut, the Short Ugly People Who Fornicate with Bears would move even deeper into their forbidding mountains. They carried huge nets made of plaited cloth and weighty ropes woven from strips of fur. Beyond the Far Passes, cloaked from any prying eye, hidden in glacial caves and rocky burrows, they would find the Great Bears of the Iron Mountains. These were the most feared animals in the Known Continent.

As tall as two Northmen standing one on the other's shoulders, covered with a shaggy hide that resisted even the bolts of crossbows, weighing as much as two horses and able to outrun them, with claws like stabbing swords and teeth like daggers, these beasts feared no other living thing. Yet, every spring when the Short Ugly People Who Fornicate with Bears would return from the mountains, they would bring back such a bear, in captivity.

Her mouth muzzled, her limbs bound, her great

claws wrapped in layer after layer of protective fur, the Great She-Bear would be carried down from the mountains and into the village. No one knew how she was captured. No one knew how many lives were lost. No one knew how these lumpy little brutes could even carry such a beast.

When the muzzled monster was brought to the village a three-day ceremony followed, with much guzzling of potions and chanting by the fire. After three days of dancing, grunting, and drum-beating the men who could still stand formed a line. One by one, they mounted the captive She-Bear and spent their seed inside her.

When the entire tribe was thus satiated, the Great Bear was released. Some Bears turned on the tribe and wreaked havoc. Some Bears stumbled away.

This foul ritual was the source of the tribe's power, strength, and reputation. For no wise man makes an enemy of anyone who can fornicate with a bear.

Halberd was intrigued by the Short Ugly People. For years tales told at the hearth celebrated the ability of their shaman, Fallat. Fallat could travel by dreams, conjure demons from the air, brew the fearsome poison that coated their arrowheads, and even, the Northmen grandfathers whispered, will himself into a trance state whence he visited the dreams of others. This, the grandfathers said, exhibited the most potent mystical power on earth.

When Halberd reached young manhood he determined to seek out Fallat. Since childhood Halberd had known things others did not. He knew which years crops would be good and where rich villages for plundering lay. He could cure his father of winter chills and his brothers of their wounds.

Halberd had the gift of prophecy.

The core of Halberd's power lay in the Dream World.

Halberd traveled many places in his dreams. He beheld the future of other tribes and the past of his own. He gained great wisdom from his visions, but he seldom understood all that he was taught. He could not pierce the veil of his own future. He could offer knowledge to others, but not himself.

The Vikings respected the mystical and lived in a world ruled by many capricious gods. They believed each man had a task on earth, and that not every man could fulfill every job. Great seers were not expected to fight, but to spend their lives with spells and potions, communing with the gods, aiding their villages or tribes.

Halberd longed for battle and adventure. The village priest found him too rambunctious and interested in the sword. When Halberd tired of grinding up herbs and taking orders, he left the priest's employ. Alone, Halberd's power increased. Halberd understood that the village priest had not a tenth of his vision. The priest had dominated him so no one might learn.

Halberd knew he must find a Master of Dreams. Halberd decided to apprentice himself to Fallat, Seer of the Short Ugly People. Fallat would know secrets long forgotten by a tribe as civilized as the Northmen.

Halberd went to his father to tell him of his journey. As usual his father, Danyeel, a village elder and Tribal Judge, sat in his Judge's Chair, hearing the complaints of two neighboring farmers. Halberd waited patiently for his father to finish.

As Tribal Judge, Danyeel commanded much respect. Though he had never been a warrior or raider, never possessed a sword or battleax, he was feared throughout the Northland. Danyeel was the most sarcastic man for hundreds of leagues. His acid tongue and cutting words of scorn had flailed every man he had ever met. Yet no man ever challenged the insults which Danyeel flung. Danyeel had a formidable wit. He also carried a tiny razor-sharp dagger in his cloak at all times.

It was said that over the years Danyeel had disemboweled five of his enemies. No one ever saw Danyeel make a thrust with his knife, and no victim's family ever brought a complaint against him. All five had visited or been visited by Danyeel for the resolution of some quarrel with him. Several hours after each visit their stomachs had fallen open and their guts had spilled to the floor.

Danyeel, the stories claimed, was so adroit with his blade that he could perfectly place a slash in each man's stomach. This nick, rendered so delicately that no man felt it, would spring open hours later and dump the victim's life in glistening coils onto his own feet. Every dead man bore a small slash on the front of his clothes. Every dead man had seen Danyeel. But two of the five had been in the company of others, and these witnesses had seen no assault. From Danyeel had Halberd inherited his lightning-quick sword arm and keen mind.

It was easier to bear Danyeel's insults than to test the legend. And, in truth, when Danyeel was calm his counsel was wise. If he respected the man he was counseling. Woe to him whom Danyeel despised, for in exchange for sound advice a man would pay dearly.

"If I must listen to that fool," Danyeel would say, "I'll be well compensated."

Halberd disliked his father's outbursts, but he was accustomed to them. He had no fear of this great red-bearded loudmouth.

When Danyeel had given his opinion in the matter before him, part of which suggested that one of the complainants would be better off if he never again attempted to think for himself, Danyeel turned to his waiting son.

"So, Halberd?" he roared. "Are you here for gold? I have none to give you. Your brother Valdane has taken it all."

Halberd told his father of his plan to visit Fallatt. Danyeel shook his head and sat silently for a long time.

"You, Halberd, are the seventh son, as was I," Danyeel began. "You were born with special gifts, as I was not. You were born for the mystical life. With no inheritance due you, you will wander. Adventure and battle will be your lot, no doubt. And why not? It is our way.

"You will have no land, no serfs, no sheep. All these will go to Valdane. Perhaps your destiny lies with Fallat. His power is far greater than ours. He has protected those savages of his for many generations. He is older than any living man, and no Great-Grandfather can recall the story of the day of his birth. Fallat has always been among us. You cannot comprehend his power. Few Northman have even tried.

"But perhaps he is lonely. Surely no one among those Bear-Defilers could ever learn what he might teach. He will know you are coming before you draw near. Perhaps he will tell his warriors not to eat you for supper. Perhaps.

"If you must make this quest, then go, my son. But beware. I do not believe Fallat wants to teach you. He will only use you as some test of his powers, some object for revenge. Nothing he tells you will be as it is. He is a fiend."

Danyeel sat, his red-haired hands clasped over his enormous belly. He sighed and straightened his back, gazing over Halberd's head to the sea. He had nothing more to say.

Halberd went inside the stone lodge house to say goodbye to his mother. Thessah, the tribal storyteller, knew all the secrets of all the families that formed their village. Thessah kept the ancient myths alive and adjudicated disputes among the women of the village and the Gods of Aasgard and Midgard. Thessah understood when to pray to Thor and when to Loki, when to ask for assistance from Freyja and when to beg Odin for his intervention.

Thessah saw the power that Halberd possessed.

She taught him not only the gods of the Northman but also the ways of worship of other tribes. From Thessah Halberd inherited his love of the spoken word and his knowledge of the religious workings of other worlds, both mortal and immortal.

Thessah knew Halberd would leave. Not for a raid lasting a day, a month, or even a year. But forever. She wanted him to be prepared. Halberd drew her to him.

"Mother," he said, "I'm leaving. I must go to the Iron Mountains."

Thessah gazed at him calmly. "Beware Fallat," she said. "Remember, he worships only Loki, the Trickster. As a follower of the Devious One he is constrained to be polite. His manners will be perfect. Ignore the barbarians around him and accept his hospitality. Only that will protect you."

"How do you know my destination?" Halberd was amazed.

"I have ears and your father shouts." Thessah smiled at her son as if to remind him that she, too, had her gifts. Thessah had no need of eavesdropping. She could hear things that were never said. She could hear the thoughts in Halberd's head. She always could.

"Who is Fallat, then? Is he not one of the Short Ugly People?"

"Fallat," Thessah answered, "is a servant of Loki. He has held many forms over many years. The Short Ugly People worship him. Fallat knows if he takes their form the Known World will ignore him. He is too clever to want earthly power. He is not vain enough to need it. All he craves is knowledge. Dark knowledge. If he takes you in it will be to steal your power. Fear him."

Halberd left that day, trudging east. By dragonhead ship he sailed across the fjords and bays of his own territory. When the ship landed he was on the eastern shore of the Great Forest, that ocean of trees which stretched to the Endless Steppes, over which the Mongols rode. Halberd had been as far as the Steppes. He knew the Great Forest well.

Days of walking north and east brought him to the first passes which led to the Iron Mountains. Here the forest gradually thinned, replaced by gray slopes of boulders, crashing mountain streams, and towering black cliffs. As the mountains shut out the sky behind him, clouds closed in. Rain hung close to his head and the rock trails grew slick.

Gone was the huge evergreen forest, replaced as he climbed by stunted leafless dwarfs struggling upward through the cracks in the black rock.

Soon no trees grew near the rocky path. The black mountains leaned over Halberd, throwing rain on him with every step. And though he showed no sign of noticing, the Short Ugly People Who Fornicate with Bears were all around him.

He could smell them as he walked and hear their mumbled gibberish from behind the boulders that shielded them. They were Fallat's spies. Halberd knew Fallat was aware of his approach. At night, when Halberd was wrapped in his furs, strange beings came into his dreams: Great Bears who bore flowers, distant ancestors of the Short Ugly People who carried clubs and ate their enemies alive, and a pair of black, glowing eyes. The eyes, attached to no face, hovered in space, watching him calmly, measuring him. Halberd knew the apparitions were sent by Fallat. The eyes that never blinked could belong to no one else.

Halberd felt some fear, but he sensed that Fallat was protecting him from the Short Ugly People. Only a few leagues separated Halberd from the last known location of their major camp. If the Short Ugly People wanted him dead they could have killed him anytime. They were allowing Halberd to approach.

Lonely in his damp furs before sleep, Halberd almost prayed. He would not pray to Odin, god of the rich, the landed, and the firstborn. No, Odin was not interested in Halberd's plight. Instead, Halberd thought only of Thor, bringer of order, protector of the needy, Master of the Hammer. If Halberd needed a steadying hand, he needed Thor's.

As the force of Fallat's presence grew stronger, Halberd also thought of Loki, Fallat's Master. Halberd would need all of Thor's firm, clear guidance to deal with Loki's tricks.

On the third morning of dark rock, seeping rain, and low black clouds, Fallat bid Halberd welcome.

Deep grunts awakened Halberd. Though he ached to grab his sword and leap to his feet, Halberd forced himself to lie still. Slowly he opened his eyes. The blackened tip of a fire-hardened wooden spear poked an inch from his nose. Oozing slime coated the sharp point. Surrounding Halberd were eight or ten of the Short Ugly People, all holding spears against the fur of his sleeping roll.

They bound Halberd's arms quickly and led him off at the end of a rope. Taken from him were his leather and bronze shield, his leather armor, his great Goth two-handed broadsword with its wondrous silver-encrusted handle, the three-sided stabbing dirk he wore horizontally behind his back, and finally his battleax, the vicious iron-headed serpent he had carried since his first raid.

The Short Ugly People stayed a good distance from Halberd. Their stench was overwhelming, and Halberd had to assume that to their nostrils he stank as well. Halberd, though only of average height for a Northman, towered over the Short Ugly People. His flaming red hair and thick red beard posed no novelty to them. They had raided all over the Great Forest and knew many different tribes.

After hours of stumbling over the rocky path, Halberd was yanked off the trail into a tiny vertical cleft in the rock wall of a basalt mountain. It was near the end of the day. The Short Ugly People moved through this invisible opening with ease, but the low height and narrow walls forced Halberd to turn sideways and bend over. Once through this crack Halberd stood in a hidden glade, surrounded by high rock walls.

Caves honeycombed the cliffs, and the thin trickle of a fresh mountain stream ran through the middle of the glade. At the base of the cliff, under the caves, was a vast pile of bones, reaching higher in the air than any three Short Ugly People. Many of the bones were human.

Next to the bone pile was an ash heap of rusted swords, broken lance points, crushed helmets, and blood-drenched singlets. The Short Ugly People could have armed a rabble from this pile, but they liked their stone arrowheads and wooden spears. They never trusted metal arms. The black dirt around the stream appeared to be paved with round smooth white stones. Looking closer, Halberd saw these were skulls set deeply into the earth.

At the base of the cliffs, beside a network of ladders than ran to the various caves, stood a tent made from a bear hide that had been scraped clean of hair. As large as any Northman lodge house, the tent showed no markings, no decorations, nothing to identify its occupant. Halberd waited calmly, taking in the camp and all its details, which no living man from another tribe had ever described.

The tent flap was flung aside. A man emerged, but, to Halberd's disappointment, he appeared to be an ordinary member of his tribe. As the man stepped up to Halberd and stared into his eyes, Halberd feared for his life. Judging from the fearful step backward every Short Ugly Person took when the man emerged from his tent, this was Fallat. But Fallat had no special wisdom shining in his eyes, no deep understanding etched in his sloping, hatchetlike face. The black, watchful eyes from the dreams were not the eyes in this primitive's face. Was Fallat just another savage? If so, then Halberd was just another meal. Halberd watched Fallat carefully. Perhaps the shaman was too clever to show his cleverness.

After a moment, Fallat barked an order to his men in the grunting incomprehensible snorts of the Short Ugly People. Two ran forward and, using a heavy stone knife, cut the ropes that bound Halberd's hands. Two more dropped his weapons at his feet. Fallat gestured for him to put them on.

Expecting now to fight for his life, Halberd picked his weapons up carefully. The broadsword went into the sheath which hung over his left shoulder. The silver-encrusted handle protruded above his head, ready for him to reach up and swing it into action. The battleax slid into its holster on his left hip. Halberd's three-sided dagger went into a horizontal scabbard sewn into his leather armor. The knife rested just above his hips. Finally he fitted his shield carefully onto his left forearm and nodded at Fallat. He was ready for combat.

"Quite formidable, young Northman," Fallat said in a relaxed and colloquial use of the Viking tongue. "But all those arms are not required for you to subdue your meal. It is already dead." Fallat turned and strode to his tent.

Halberd stood rooted to the earth with shock. "How do you know our tongue?" he asked, keeping his voice detached with great effort.

"I know all the languages of the Known World and many from the Giants and the Dwarves. I know all of what you have come seeking to learn.

Now, we dine." Fallat gestured Halberd into his tent.

Remembering Thessah's words, remembering that Fallat, as a servant of Loki, was required to be hospitable, Halberd followed the shaman into the tent. The food was simple: meat burned at a fire and roots dug from the rocks.

"Why do you remain among these people?" Halberd asked, when the meal was done. "A man of your knowledge could be anywhere in the Known World."

"I live here to be left to do as I please," Fallat replied. "I protect my warriors and they follow my orders. Here I have no rivals. But here also, there is no one who shares my gifts. No one else may travel with me to the Dream World. No one can discuss with me what I have learned.

"But you might be that person. You may well have the power to understand what I can teach. You might have the power to see into your dreams, and perhaps even the dreams of others."

Halberd looked around the tent. There were no books or manuscripts, no tools or altars. There was only a small likeness of Loki on a tree stump. It did not appear to be the home of a great shaman. Still, his father feared this man. Surely all this flattery led to some deceit.

"Pay closer attention," Fallat hissed. "Look not for earthly wealth, but for power, look at one who does not require possessions or written words. I carry my knowledge in my head, and I take this knowledge from the Dream World."

"What world is that?"

"It is the world which resides near the Waking

World, and the door to it opens only when we sleep. In it lies all the wisdom you hope to gain."

Fallat said nothing more for some time. The sky grew dark. The tent walls were thin, but Halberd heard no sound from the camp. Rising from the hard-dirt floor of the tent, he peered out the doorway. There were no Short Ugly People to be seen.

"From time to time men of other tribes have sought me here," Fallat said. "When they do my warriors run to their caves and hide. They fear the magic of any stranger."

So, others had taken this trek before him. Where were they today? If they had lived, perhaps Halberd would have heard of them. Perhaps none had survived. Halberd had felt a bit foolish, sitting bedecked with arms on the dirt floor of a tent next to a small savage man wearing skins, but he did not relinquish his guard. The two sat in silence as the night grew darker.

"I must sleep, now," Fallat said. "Your sleeping furs are outside. Perhaps you will learn something of the Dream World tonight."

Halberd left the tent. The night was clammy and damp. Thick clouds hung over the rocky glade, blotting out the moon and stars. The Short Ugly People were all in caves. He saw no one. There was no sound but the creek. Halberd wrapped himself in his furs and slept.

He was walking on a narrow path in a dense forest. Trees overhung the path, and thorns formed a wall on either side. From around the next bend in the path he heard the full-throated growl of a Great She-Bear. She was moving toward him. He reached over his shoulder for his sword. It was gone! He was unarmed. The bear stepped into view. She was no more than ten paces away. In a moment she would attack. Halberd took a backward step. The Great She-Bear bent low, ready to explode forward at his slightest motion. Her teeth were green and mossy, her coat was slathered with sweat, and her chest was crosshatched with the scars of spears and swords that had failed to kill her. Her claws, longer than Halberd's hands, gleamed in the bright sun like razors. Gazing into her black, black eyes, Halberd knew he had only seconds to live. He also, finally, recognized the watchful eyes from his earlier dreams.

Halberd wrenched himself awake. He knew the Bear was still there, and that his life would be over in moments. Throwing off his furs, he seized his broadsword and shook off the scabbard. Halberd jumped to his feet and ran to Fallat's tent. Through the hide wall he could see a lantern burning brightly. Its glow outlined Fallat lying on his bedframe, deep in a trance-sleep.

Halberd raised his sword over his head. The keen blade threw glints of lanternlight over Fallet's tent wall. Halberd brought the sword down with all his strength. The blade, heavy and sharp, sliced through the wall of the tent with no resistance. Likewise it passed through the thick wood of Fallat's bedframe. Any blade sharp and heavy enough to slash through tent and sturdy oak without pause would be given little trouble by the scrawny neck and matted hair of a duplicitous Shaman. Fallat's severed head sailed across the tent and chunked heavily into the earthen floor.

As Fallat's head bounced off the hard-packed dirt, an animal howl of anguish sounded from every cave in the cliff. The Short Ugly People came boiling down the scaffolding, ready to tear Halberd to pieces. Halberd jumped through the slit in the tent wall and grabbed Fallat's head by its long dark hair.

Holding the bleeding head at arm's length, Halberd shoved it out the tent-flap door. With a collective gasp of fear, the Short Ugly People fell back. Without pulling the head back inside, Halberd swiveled around to scan the tent for booty. The only object other than the severed bed was an odd amber-colored jewel resting on a taut-stretched piece of bear fur atop a tripod of sticks. The jewel glowed brightly, lit by an inner fire. Fallat had concealed this jewel from Halberd, so it must have power. Halberd had never seen anything like it. Halberd leaned as far into the tent as he could stretch, balancing on tiptoe to keep the Shaman's head sticking out the tent flap.

He grabbed the jewel.

Though it glowed, it gave off no heat. Halberd dropped the amber egg into his leather armor.

He stepped out of the tent, bearing the head before him. The tent was surrounded. At the sight of Fallat's head, his mouth hanging open, the bloody strands dribbling from where his neck used to be, the Short Ugly People dropped their weapons and fell to one knee, their heads bowed. Halberd sheathed his broadsword and warily reached for a dropped spear. Not one of the hairy little cannibals moved. Halberd seized a spear and backed slowly to the narrow gap in the rock wall, holding the dead shaman's head toward the prostrate primitives. Hunching over, he dashed through the crevice, not caring as the head banged off the rock walls. Once outside, on the path, he took a deep breath for the first time since the bear had appeared in his dream.

The clouds were lifting above him, and thin slivers of moonlight showed the rocky path. Halberd set the head beside him and broke the spear in half. He then jammed Fallat's head onto the poison-smeared point and wedged the spear, butt-first, into his armor next to his shoulder-mounted broadsword scabbard. The shaman's head, carried high above Halberd's and facing backward, swayed in the moonlight with each step. That, thought Halberd, should keep any pursuing Short Ugly People at bay.

But shortly after turning his back on the cleft in the rock, Halberd heard a loud fluttering aimed right at his head. He whirled quickly, his shield arm up, his battleax in his hand. The speed of his turn sent Fallat's head sailing off the spear. It hit the path with a soggy thump and rolled under a large boulder.

Halberd saw nothing. He waited, watching for a poisoned spear or dripping arrow to come whizzing out of the predawn darkness.

A voice spoke, right into his ear.

"Calm yourself, Northman. We mean you no harm."

Halberd leaped aside and swung at the voice

with all his might. His ax cut only air. He crouched, ax up, searching the darkness. The voice laughed.

Two ravens hopped cockily out of the shadows. They came boldly to Halberd's feet and stared up at him, turning their heads this way and that. The larger one spoke again.

"We are Odin's servants, come to pick the brains of the dead magician. We must hurry or Loki's messengers will beat us to it. We cannot find the head. Where is it? Why did you throw it away?"

"I didn't throw it anywhere," Halberd gasped. "I think it went under that rock. Besides, you cannot have the head. I need it to protect myself from the Short Ugly People Who Fornicate with Bears."

"Keep it then, brave warrior. We do not care where it goes. We will accompany you."

At last Halberd recognized these birds. They were Huggin and Munin, messengers of Odin. They picked the skulls of the dead and near-dead, learning all that the skulls contained. This knowledge they swiftly communicated to Odin, Lord of Aasgard. By this intelligence he maintained his omnipotence and his appearance of knowing all things before they happened. The ravens had great knowledge themselves.

"You may accompany me," Halberd declared, "only if you reveal to me the mystery of this stone." Halberd pulled the jewel from his armor. The glow had faded. The ravens studied it carefully and looked at one another before the larger one answered.

"Apparently you will be a great shaman. You

have seized the Jewel of Kyrwyn-Coyne. It is used by those who travel to the Dream World. More you must learn for yourself. However, the Jewel is not evil. It is a tool, to be used for good or not depending on the disposition of the owner. It carries no curse. It will not taint you."

Relieved, Halberd retrieved the somewhat battered head and stuck it back on the spear. The ravens climbed onto his shoulder and began to peck at the skull. Halberd barely heard the scratchy sound of their feet or the moist whacks of their beaks on the leaky skull. As he negotiated the dangerous path in the light of the rising sun he was deep in thought. Fallat had sought to teach him a lesson, a lesson in power that would have ended Halberd's life. Fallat was not so powerful as he had believed he was, but great lessons he had given Halberd. Halberd had learned four critical things:

For those with the Gift and the Power, the Dream World never stopped. Whatever events were set in motion there continued while the dreamer was awake, just as events in the Waking World continued while one slept. One merely visited the Dream World, one did not control it.

The greatest power was the ability to project oneself or one's servants into the dreams of others. Fallat could do this at will. Halberd still had to learn how. He would not be strong enough to battle other shamans in the Dream World until he learned.

Any shaman, no matter how powerful, could be defeated by any other. Halberd must never underestimate any enemy.

Finally, Halberd had learned that if one cannot defeat the magic, one should cut off the head of the magician.

His memories faded. The image of the rocky path and pecking ravens disappeared. He was back in his dark stone house. The snow blew hard outside. It was drifted higher than the door. Halberd would not get out until morning.

His meditations had served him well. He felt strong and ready for battle, in this or any other world. His grief would fuel him, not rule him. Come morning, Halberd would make his way through the head-high drifts and find Usuthu. Together they would equip a band of hardy fools and sail to the icy Edge of the Earth in the dead of winter. Valdane would be avenged.

Usuthu

The storm ended by sunrise. Halberd chopped at the snow frozen above the height of his door and clambered out into the drifts. Sinking to his knees with every step, he began the long trudge to Usuthu's yurt.

Usuthu lived in a round tent set on a wooden frame. In it he worshiped his gods, primarily the fearsome Bahaab Dahaabs, who demanded sacrifices of his worshiper's blood, spilled in battle and in conquest. Though initially regarded as a demon, Usuthu had gradually been accepted into Halberd's village. Though his magic was strong, he offered to share it with no one but Halberd. This was only fitting. They were, after all, brothers.

Not brothers by blood, but of spirit. From the end of the first day of their acquaintance they knew their souls had been partners for centuries. Usuthu was Halberd's strong right arm, and Halberd was Usuthu's.

Halberd slogged on through the snow, past the forbidding trees, occasionally passing a stone house shut fast against the cold. The sun had barely risen above the trees, and the snow's crunchy surface broke beneath each step. Though his body struggled with the drifts, his mind drifted to another time.

The trick of immersing himself in memory had been learned from Thessah at an early age. All Northmen must endure hardship and privation, howling seas and bitter winds, unbearable cold and killing isolation. To escape the tedium which accompanied these dangers, and killed just as surely, Halberd's memories became a sanctuary.

Now, as he sank into the frozen snow and the icy wind lashed at his cloak, his mind, set free, relived the journey that had united him with his spirit brother, Usuthu.

Some months after his return from the land of the Short Ugly People, Halberd had built his own stone house some distance from his father's. Using the booty seized from several raids against the Heathmen to the west, he had paid workers to drag the stones and raise the walls and roof. In this house he began to regularly visit the Dream World, trusting to his instincts and the Jewel of Kyrwyn-Coyne for protection. As his understanding of the Dream World grew, so did his faith in his ability to prophesy.

Hence he was prepared when his father and brothers appeared one morning at his house. They sat astride their muscular ponies, dressed for voyage and combat.

"Halberd," Danyeel shouted as always, "make yourself ready. A great adventure has been revealed to us by our scouts, and we have several days' journey ahead of us."

"Father," replied Halberd, "I am ready."

The voyage, though not its purpose, had been revealed to Halberd in his sleep the night before.

Halberd brought his pony from the animal shed. All his gear was strapped to the animal. His brothers looked at one another with eyebrows upraised. Only Valdane and Danyeel seemed unsurprised.

"Yes, little brother, you have a great gift. I'd sooner have you by my side than any of these older buffoons. Ride next to me."

Halberd pulled abreast with his favorite brother, Valdane, at the head of the column. Valdane wheeled his pony about and led the family off toward the bay.

The ponies were put aboard one dragonhead ship, with three of the brothers on board to watch over Danyeel's serfs, who would row and watch the vessels while Danyeel and his sons traveled inland. These serfs were mostly warriors captured by Danyeel's sons in battle, then given to the old man. These voyages supplied the only joy in their hard lives. The chance of a good fight was their reward.

Danyeel, Halberd, Valdane, and two middle brothers, Labrans and Mahvreeds, boarded the lighter, more responsive warship with a fighting crew of eight. The boats were rapidly loaded with casks of water, dried meat, fish, and barrels of mead. Any other food they required they would steal from whoever was sufficiently unwise as to cross their path.

They settled into their places behind the oars, with Valdane the captain of one ship and Janor the Insane, a mystic warrior who never stopped talking, at the tiller of the other. Few could understand what Janor said, but his prowess at the tiller through storm or shallows was unequaled. Everyone prepared to row except Danyeel, who never worked, rowed, or fought. Danyeel would roam the ship, preaching the superiority of the Northman as a fighting man.

They slipped their harbor, heading south and east, across the great bay to the northern edge of the Known Continent. It was a bright summer day, warm and humid. The breeze came fresh, blowing from the north, and filled the sail. Painted on the sail, now displayed by the wind, was the proud crest of Danyeel, a hawk striking a leaping fish, showing their name and purpose for all to see.

As the ships leaped from wave to wave, Danyeel walked from one end of the dragonhead ship to the other, swaying with the sea with every step and declaiming at the top of his lungs.

"No other tribe or village or people can do what we do, my sons, no one. No one on the face of this World has our ships or gods. The gods love us because our ships are strong and we are unafraid. We are unafraid because the gods love us and our ships are strong. The World is as it should be! Think of it. The slavers of the Land of Sand on the Inland Sea have boats which draw almost no water, so they may sail into whatever town they like, to buy and sell their human cargo. But if they are caught in a storm, they are lost.

"The pirates of the Northern Tribes have stout ships which may sail the great Northern Sea in any storm, but they draw too much water to raid any shallow port. But . . . the dragon ships, my boys, the dragon ships alone can sail in one foot of water or broach a storm when the waves tower overhead. Of all the raiders in the World, none have our ships. None may go where we go! None have our freedom."

Though Danyeel made this speech each time he went raiding, his sons still filled with pride and the lust for blood that ran when the waves were small and the wind behind them. With the wind so strong, all oars were shipped. Only the helmsman worked now.

"Tell me of this great army we travel to see, Father," Halberd asked Danyeel as they sat on the lee gunwale and watched the waves shoot past.

"They are the Mongols, my son, the tribes which command the Great Steppes to the east even as we rule the sea. And they are much like us, only their ships are horses. They ride where they please and strike as they please. They are fearsome warriors. My scouts tell me there are more of them massed on the Blue River than any army ever seen in the Known Continent. More, they say, than the Men of the Short Swords who came from the south many centuries ago."

"Will we fight them, Father?" asked Valdane.

"By the Giants and Dwarves I pray we do not. There are more of them than you can imagine, and every one a brave man. But they do not seek our territory. We travel so we may see them, because we cannot see something like this every day. And if we find a good fight along the way, so much the better."

Valdane and Halberd looked at one another

and shrugged. It was often so. Danyeel wanted an adventure, and now he had one. Great armies were nothing new to the Northmen.

After two days' sail they reached the northern mouth of the Odra River. After taking the ponies ashore for grass and exercise they found a small party of unarmed men near their boats. Beside the men was a large mountain of stores.

"Brave Northmen," began the eldest of the men, "we have no quarrel with you and wish you well on your journey. If you could but spare our poor village . . ." He swept his hand to indicate a rocky fortress looming over the mouth of the river.

"Quiet, fool," barked Danyeel. "We won't waste ourselves on your castle, and we don't want all this food. Labrans, take half of this pile and let these cowards drag home the rest."

The food was quickly stored and the men departed. Valdane whispered to Halberd as they rowed down the river, "Doubtless every archer in that pile of rock was trained on our heads. Still, I'd rather fight than take tribute, but Danyeel has somewhere he wants to be."

And so it went as they wound their way down through the heart of the Continent. Villages and fortresses, towns and captains of small armies would appear offering food and shelter, always at some distance from the town in question. When the Vikings neared the Great Walled City which marks the change from the Odra River to the Blue River, Danyeel was struck by the absence of armies or fighting men.

"I could have the eyes of Heimdall and still I

would be blind. I am truly a fool. Now I understand why everyone wants to avoid a fight. The armies are all preparing for the Mongols. There must be more of them than I thought. We won't risk the hospitality of the Great Walled City. Let us hide our boats here until the sun has set."

The Northmen guided their boats under overhanging trees on the west side of the Odra River. Above them towered the high black rock walls of the city. Guards patrolled her battlements, and the steps which led to her wharfs were protected by high walls. The wharfs themselves were safe inside huge gates. Here the river was so wide the Northmen could barely make out the other side. Men lived their lives without ever crossing this river, they were born, grew up, and died without even leaving their villages, and here, in their midst, hidden and fearless, were men who had seen the World, men who went where they pleased.

Darkness fell, and soon the only light flickered in the lanterns of the Walled City, the biggest and most protected city in the Known Continent. Its glow lit up the sky. But though light it was, its very brightness blinded any guards who might stare into the dark. Safe in the cloak of night, the Northmen pushed off and drifted silently to the middle of the river. There, in pitch blackness, they rowed around the Great City and into the mouth of the Blue River.

By dawn they were leagues beyond the city and into the open, flat farmlands of the Continent. The Northmen hated these peasants and their armored rulers. The country was ripe for the plucking. Unlike the Odra River, the Blue River was not lined with cliffs but with flat, rolling farmland or gentle cut banks. The Vikings could see for leagues beyond the riverbanks.

As the day wore on they noticed more and more soldiers on the western bank. Oddly, these were soldiers of many different lands and different tribes, different rulers and different allegiances. If, in all their milling and dust-raising, they noticed the Northmen dragon ships in the middle of the great river, they gave no sign. By dark the banks were jammed with armies and their campfires glowed as far as the eye could see. Again the Northmen stuck to the western shore, anchoring just off the protection of a high dirt bank.

Danyeel huddled with his eldest son, Valdane, and his wisest, Halberd. Janor the Insane rocked on his heels next to them, babbling as always.

"Why do you think all the armies of the Continent are massing here?" Danyeel asked his sons.

"Only because some other threat is near," Valdane answered. "Some threat that is greater than the one they pose to one another. They have not come together in these numbers in all of time, as far as I know."

"Yes, they are deeply afraid," Halberd said. "My dreams reveal to me an army on the eastern side of this river, an army the likes of which we have never seen. That, Father, is why we camp on this shore tonight, despite presence of our enemies. You fear them less than you fear what lies on the other side."

"Many horses, many horses, and many bows,"

cackled Janor, mad as always and right as usual. "Many shields and many stones, many, many heads to crack."

"But what threat could cross the Blue River?" asked Halberd. "It's wider here than some small seas."

"You see much but you don't know all," chided Danyeel. "Just a few leagues south of us this river could be jumped by a small horse or a large man."

"Not precisely, Father," chided Valdane. "It could be forded by an army, but hardly jumped across."

"Whatever," said their father. "I shall not test the will of the Norns by going so far south as that. For to see it, I think, is to die. When it's dark and we're rested, we will cross to the eastern shore and venture inland, to see their fearsome threat, whatever it may be, with our own eyes. For that reason only have I come so far."

And so they slept in their boats, as they had done for many nights past. Their ponies made not a sound and the men slept deeply, unafraid. When the night sky showed no moon, the guards awakened them. They slipped their muffled oars into the water and silently stole toward the east.

The eastern shore was overhung with trees. They ran their dragon ships right in among the branches and offloaded the ponies onto the land. Instantly two of the serfs ran up and down the bank, leading the ponies behind them. The ponies' nervous energy soon dissipated and the chariot of the sun began its journey across the sky.

"It seems deserted here, my boys," said Danyeel. "I think we may travel, at least for a little while."

The serfs were left to guard the ship. None would flee. They had been slaves before they were serfs, and Danyeel treated them as well as they could expect. All were former warriors and all possessed honor. Defeated in battle, they knew Fate had decreed that they should serve Danyeel. Besides, a chance to shed blood might arise, and that was all they lived for.

"Take the boats to the middle of the river by day, and return to this copse of trees by night," Danyeel commanded them. "Wait for us here until we return or you starve to death."

Danyeel and his seven sons loaded their ponies with provisions and mounted their fur saddles. All were weighted down with bows, arrows, lances, swords, and daggers. Only Danyeel carried no arms.

Guiding themselves by the Blue River, they trotted south. Keeping close to the riverbank and cutting inland whenever they spotted high ground, they kept a close vigil. Nothing approached them from the north, but to the south a great dust cloud was rising. As they drew nearer they were shocked by its size. It obscured the riverbank for a distance of leagues.

"Camp here tonight," said Danyeel. "I'll go no closer until I understand that cloud."

As they slept, Halberd dreamed of a black giant, a huge man with a drooping mustache and a longbow as big as the mast of a dragon ship. The giant clasped his arm in friendship and pointed with an enormous finger to the north. He was smiling.

Suddenly he was awake. Janor was shaking him roughly.

"Many fires," Janor squealed. "Too many fires!"

Halberd scrambled up the tiny knoll on which stood the rest of his brothers and his father. Below them, no more than two leagues away, was the light of thousands and thousands of campfires. The fires stretched to the horizon to the south and to the east. They easily covered an area five times as big as the Great Walled City. There was no estimating their number. It was said that there were twenty thousand souls in the Great Walled City, but Halberd, who had seen cities greater than that in the Land of Sand on the Inland Sea, knew those encamped were much greater than five times that number.

Even at this distance the ground shook from the hooves of horses. The air was clogged with smoke. The shouts and cries of this vast camp filled the predawn air. Whoever they were, they were certainly not hiding and they were certainly not afraid.

"Scouts will be all around us," whispered Mahvreeds the Cautious. "We should return to the ships."

"No, my boy," responded Danyeel jovially. "I've come this far to see these men, and I will not return until I have. We will wait."

Full dawn revealed an astounding sight. The campfires did not stretch to the riverbank. They stopped perhaps a league before it. The camp was made of round fur tents set on wooden wagons with wheels higher than a man's head. Other, larger, brightly colored tents flying long pennants stood among them. The camp was unimaginably big. The Northmen could see no end to it.

Moving slowly from the camp toward the river was one long line of mounted men. They wore round helmets of leather and steel. They bore curved swords and great bows, or long lances with double-sided blades. They rode stirrup to stirrup on husky horses that looked as indestructible as the slant-eyed men who rode them. The men had yellow skin and broad cheekbones. They were short and wide. This line of mounted warriors disappeared over the southern horizon.

"How many, Halberd?" hissed Valdane, too stunned by the sight to speak aloud.

"Well over one hundred of thousands, I believe."

"This explains the vast armies of the West," said Danyeel. "If these barbarians can cross the Blue River they will ride until they strike the Great Western Ocean. This is a sight to remember."

Even as they spoke the great army of horsemen rode to the eastern shore and gazed over its short distance to the armies of the West. There they sat, as the day wore on. From behind them, to the east, the dust cloud of camp grew and grew. It rose to the sky in a light brown cloud. It blotted the army from sight and drove Halberd and his family to wrap cloths about their eyes and noses.

"Something is brewing there," said Danyeel. "That dust covers much activity."

When darkness came the earth again shook from the pounding of hooves. The Northmen rested on their knoll, chewing dried meat and sipping mead from a flask. The ground trembled beneath them as they ate. Yet they heard no splashing, no curses, no whinnying horses trying to swim. The army from the East was not attempting to cross the river. The dust still surrounded them when they lay on the ground to sleep.

The dust had subsided by daybreak. A cloud still hung in the air, but it was leagues to the east. The army had vanished. The camp was gone. All that remained was a furrowed line of hoofprints along the riverbank that ran south until the earth met the sky.

"They've turned and gone back home," cried Danyeel. "Why? Why, by the Giants! They've deprived us of one of the greatest battles any mortal has ever seen."

"Father, let me ride to the east and scout their trail," said Labrans. "Perhaps we can learn why they have fled."

"Excellent idea, my boy. All of you will scout. I will return to the ships with Janor and have a decent meal and you boys will ride until you find out something. Travel in twos and take good care. Come, Janor."

With those words Danyeel climbed onto his pony and set off in a trot toward the ships, less than one day away. Janor hurried after him.

Halberd and Valdane set off across the dry, flat land. They were on a route farther south than any of the others, who were riding mostly east. Halberd and Valdane struck out for a small forest which sat like an island of trees in the vast sea of the desolate plain. It seemed a natural place for scouts or the rear guard of the Mongols to have camped. Perhaps they could capture one and discover why this great army had fled.

As they rode they spoke of the women in their village.

"There is none but Grettir," said Valdane. "There is none that I can see with her wit or strength."

"Nor with her beauty," said Halberd, who had thought of Grettir's flashing eyes many, many nights. Whenever she dined with them she would watch Halberd carefully from the corner of her eye. Did she know of the love he carried for her? He had to be careful, even with Valdane.

Winter was long for the Northmen. Their population was small. Close quarters bred rigid social sanctions. Infidelity was not permitted among the Northmen, and Valdane was bethrothed to Grettir. If Grettir was suspected of even flirting with Halberd it would go hard against both of them. She was not his woman. Why then did she fill his mind?

He shook his head to clear it of thoughts of her long slender neck and hard, lithe body. They were near the thick forest. Valdane would ride to the north and Halberd to the south. They would enter the trees from opposite ends.

As Halberd circled the copse of thick woods he saw it was much larger than they had first suspected. By the time he had reached the southern end he was several hours' ride from his brother. Still, he rode into the forest's cool shade without fear.

Immediately he saw that the forest had been used as a camp. Broken weapons and horse dung lay in the cool clearings. Beyond were the scraps of tents and clothing that any army leaves behind. His pony smelled the old scent of the horses here before him and shied away as Halberd prodded him onward into the forest.

He could see no sign of Valdane and did not expect to for almost a day. They were both superb trackers, he knew, and would intersect eventually. Now he must ignore any thoughts of Valdane and concentrate on the fierce premonition overcoming him.

Halberd was certain of the nearness of danger. His skin was tingling. His fist clenched and unclenched on the head of his battleax. Halberd dismounted to make himself less of a target to archers and walked next to his pony.

The bushes rustled to his right, and a Mongol sprang from cover, a short curved sword in his hand. He swung the sword downward at Halberd, who turned aside as the blade nicked the leather armor on his shoulder. The rush of the Mongol's swing carried him past Halberd, and Halberd kicked him in the lower back as he sailed by. He hit the ground and spun around toward Halberd, sword again at the ready. As he completed his turn, Halberd's battleax bit into his arm.

The Mongol dropped his sword as blood poured from his upper arm. With a grimace of pain he yanked a short stabbing knife from his belt with his left arm and slashed at Halberd. Halberd stepped nimbly backward and knocked the Mongol flat with the side of his ax.

"Where is your army?" Halberd spoke in the language of the dark slave traders from the Land of Sand on the Inland Sea. Their language, already a hodgpodge of tongues from the Southern Continent which lay below the Land of Sand, was spoken by most tribes who wandered the Known World.

The Mongol rolled for his knife and slashed at Halberd's legs, severing the fur wrappings which covered them. Enough! This was a brave man, but his life was proving too difficult to save. Halberd hopped over the swinging blade and, with a powerful sidearm stroke, crushed the Mongol's skull with the flat side of his battleax blade.

Halberd knelt over the dead warrior, offering his thanks to Thor and examining the barbarian's weapons. He was turning the short knife over in his hand when he heard an almost silent tread on the dirt behind him. Halberd whirled over onto his back, rolling away from the dead man. A sword cut into the ground where he had knelt.

Wielding the sword was the Black Giant from his dreams! There was no time for thought. Though at least a foot taller than Halberd, the giant was quicker than any man Halberd had ever seen. His sword snaked out, lashing the battleax from Halberd's hand. The ax sailed into the bushes, turning over lazily as it flew through the air.

The strength of the giant's swing carried his arm past Halberd. Halberd drew his stabbing dagger from the hidden scabbard at his back, stepped inside the arc of the giant's swing, and drove the knife toward his belly. Like lightning the giant seized Halberd's knife arm by the wrist.

The giant threw down his sword, drew his own dagger, and plunged it at Halberd's heart. Halberd grabbed the giant by the wrist, but not before the razor-sharp blade penetrated his leather armor and drew a drop of blood. Halberd could feel it trickling down his chest.

Halberd was the fastest warrior among the Northmen. No man from any tribe had ever bested him with quickness. Yet this dark giant was quicker than most animals. Halberd could not see his face. The giant towered over him. His strength was overwhelming. Halberd tried to push his own dagger in while holding back the giant's. The giant did the same to Halberd. Locked in this deadly dance, squeezing and shoving with all their might, the two warriors staggered around the clearing, both trying to gain the upper hand.

In strength they seemed to be evenly matched. Halberd had more muscle but was smaller. The giant was leaner and had much greater weight. As they shifted beneath the dappled shade, each trying to kick the feet out from under the other, Halberd studied his opponent.

Though he was the giant from the dream, he was not one of the immortal Giants who battled the gods of Aasgard. He seemed to be a full foot taller than Halberd, who was slightly over six feet tall. His skin was black, like the slave traders', but his eyes were slanted and his cheekbones broad, like the Mongols'. A drooping mustache fell over his chin. He wore a conical Mongol helmet of leather and silver and no shirt. Instead he simply wore two shields, one over his chest and another covering his back.

Halberd's arms felt paralyzed and numb. He knew he had reached the limit of his strength. He knew his muscles could not hold out much longer. He called upon his will. Halberd swore to Thor never to release this giant, unless either he or the giant was dead. He sang his vow to Thor aloud, in the proud language of the Northmen.

The giant looked down, startled at the loud bellowing, an odd look of comprehension in his slanted eyes. He too sang a loud vow, in the singsong tongue of the East. To Halberd's amazement, he understood every word.

The giant sang, "Oh Great Bahaab Dahaabs, give me strength that I might disembowel this furry monster from the North. I will not rest until this is done."

Halberd did not know the Mongol dialect, yet he understood every word. How? What sorcery was afoot? He pushed the mystery from his mind and concentrated on the sword-wrist of the giant. They had now been staggering around, locked together, for several hours.

Suddenly the giant got his foot behind Halberd's. With a heave of his leg he sent Halberd off the ground. As Halberd felt himself flung backward he yanked on the wrists of his enemy. The unexpected shift of weight drew the giant off his feet and the two sailed in the air. They hit the root-covered forest floor with a crash that shook the trees.

Yet neither relinquished his hold on the other's wrists. And neither slackened the force of his dagger against the other's chest. Now they had to be doubly wary. If one could hook his leg between the legs of his rival, he might throw the other over. Neither could risk that. They swung on their sides, pulling their legs as far from the other as possible.

And so they lay as darkness fell, locked together like sparring elk, their horns entangled so that both would starve to death. Halberd would not loosen his grip and the giant showed no sign of weakening. The sun finished its ride across the sky and the stars emerged. The moon followed and fell from the heavens. Still they lay on the dusty ground beneath the cool shade of the trees.

Halberd's arms were cramping. His throat burned from thirst and his eyes were filled with dust. His lower back was a burst of pain. His legs had no blood running from them. He could not make them move.

If the giant was in equal discomfort he gave no sign. His eyes were closed and his breathing serene. His grip remained as strong as iron.

As the sun rose over the two warriors, Halberd suffered odd visions. In these visions he was sailing under a stormy sky in a laden dragonhead ship. The crew was tough and well armed, but his brothers were not among them. Tied to the mast of this ship was the giant. Beside him rested a monstrous longbow. In another vision the giant used his longbow against an odd fur-covered enemy. Halberd stood to the side and watched the giant fire his bow. In this vision, they were allies.

In his exhaustion and determination Halberd was unaware that he spoke aloud. "Oh Loki, evil shape-changer! Are you this black giant? Is this my punishment for the death of Fallat? Why do I see visions of brotherhood when my death is so near?"

At that moment the giant shifted his position. His grip was slackening. As Halberd began to press his advantage, the giant released Halberd's hand and ceased to push his dagger against Halberd's chest. Halberd shoved his own knife forward, but instinct stopped him just before the knife went under the giant's shield.

The giant dropped his knife and lay on his back, rubbing his wrists and breathing deeply. Halberd rose to his hands and knees, trying to drive the pain out of his lower back and to locate his battleax. The giant was no longer a threat.

When the giant spoke it was in the language of the Mongols, yet once more Halberd understood every word.

"I am Usuthu," the barbarian said. "Clearly we are bothers, for I understand your language even though I have never heard it. We are matched in strength though no man is as strong as I, and we are matched in spirit.

"I believe you are the lost brother of my birth-prophecy. I cannot harm you and I will not. Our future in battle is as partners, not as enemies."

Halberd shook his legs to bring the blood back to them and stood. The giant lay on his back, at ease. The giant extended a huge hand to Halberd. Clasping Usuthu about the wrist in a grip of brotherhood, Halberd helped him to his feet.

"I believe you are right," Halberd said. "You have appeared in my dreams and I think we are destined to be warriors together."

They embraced.

Over Usuthu's shoulder, at the edge of the clearing, Halberd saw the shadowy figure of a horseman. Drawing the sword from his shoulder scabbard, he advanced on the figure.

A familiar laugh stopped him. "Relax, my brother," chuckled Valdane. "I doubt you have the strength left to even lift that sword, let alone swing it."

Halberd saw that Valdane held his bow with an arrow to the string. His eyes were bleary and rimmed with red.

"How long have you been here?"

"Since the moon rose," replied Valdane. "I've had my arrow trained on this giant since then. I knew he could not kill you. I wanted to see what would happen. Who is this black man? Is he mortal? How do you know his language? What did he say to you?"

"He," said Halberd proudly, "is my new brother."

"Well then," Valdane said, reaching for a flask of water, "call your new brother over for a drink. My throat is parched from watching you two all night."

As they stood beside Valdane's horse and quenched their thirst, Usuthu told his tale.

His mother was a black slave, brought from the Southern Continent, from the Land Where It Is Always Warm, where she had been captured by the slave traders from the Land of Sand. Carried many leagues over the sea to the Land of the Warm Forests, where not even the Northmen had been, she was sold to the Mongols and from there transported to the Eastern Castle of the Mongols, to the Court of the Great Khan.

The Great Khan ruled all the Mongols from the Eastern Palace. He awarded the tall black slave to Usuthu's father, a great Mongol war-chief. Usuthu had been born on the Great Steppes, where his father felt most at home. Though taller than any man he had ever seen, almost twice as tall as his father, Usuthu claimed to be shorter than his mother.

The huge army of Mongols had returned to the East because the Great Khan was dead. The army was well over one hundred thousand cavalry and twice that many wives and children and old men. Though the Khan was thousands and thousands of leagues away, the horse couriers of his court had reached the army in less than two weeks. Such was the power of the Khan.

When the army received the sad news and made ready to return to the Eastern Palace, Usuthu had told his father he would not be going back. It was time for his vision quest. It was time for Usuthu to fast and go without sleep, to live alone and deprived until his vision appeared and revealed his fate to him. Usually this vision was a hallucination. It would be studied by the elders around the fire. From these learned heads would come the interpretation of Usuthu's future.

In this case, however, little interpretation was needed. Halberd had appeared instead of a vision. At first Usuthu had thought that Halberd was a demon, sent to test him. Once he understood that Halberd was another human being, even if he was not a Mongol, Usuthu knew that Halberd himself was the vision.

He dedicated his allegiance to Halberd and offered his lifelong loyalty. Halberd invited him to return to the Northern Lands with his family and live his life among the snow and fjords of the Northmen.

"Indeed," said Usuthu, "this is my destiny. Where you go, I shall go. Your enemies will be mine and I will look to you for aid in my own struggles."

"What did he say?" asked Valdane.

"This is how it will be, my brother," said Usuthu. "I will not speak in your language. You alone will understand me. Also, speak to me not of your gods. I have my own."

With that Usuthu set off into the forest to find his pony. When he had found her, the three rode out of the clearing and back to the ship. Here arose Usuthu's only difficulty with the Northman way of life. He was terrified of water. His horse gladly went aboard with the others, but Usuthu at first offered to ride along the riverbank next to the ship.

When Halberd explained the impossibility of that, Usuthu said he would ride on the ship, but only if he was tied to the mast. He said he could not bear to see the wall of the ship move up and down and so wanted to face only forward. His wish was granted.

Usuthu neither slept nor ate while tied to the mast. He did not seem to notice the cold spray breaking over him, and though obviously petrified, he was never once sick. For a man who had never seen this much water, let alone sailed upon it, Usuthu adjusted well. His strength and stoicism were amazing even to a group of men as inured as Halberd's family.

Danyeel welcomed Usuthu as a son. Janor the Insane was happy to have someone new to babble to, even a seven-foot black giant. Halberd's brothers, with the exception of Valdane, regarded Usuthu with awe and suspicion, as did everyone in Halberd's village. This awe grew when the Northmen discovered that Usuthu could shoot an arrow twice as far as the strongest man in the village. None could even string his great longbow. While this made him greatly desired as a partner on hunts or raids, it also inspired jealousy.

Further jealousy was inspired by his toughness. Bred to live in the saddle, Usuthu ignored weather. No matter how deep the snow or harsh the winds, Usuthu wore his two shields front and back, leather leggings, and Mongol fur-wrapped boots. He never required a cloak and he never complained of the cold. His prowess as a horsemen far outstripped that of the Northmen, who were not that interested in riding. Only Usuthu's fear of the water made him seem mortal to the villagers, who regarded him always as a trickster, sent by the Giants who seek to destroy Aasgard.

Halberd and Usuthu became the brothers they were destined to be. Though Usuthu never entered the Dream World, his magic was potent. Bahaab Dahaabs smiled upon Usuthu and made him not only bigger, faster, and stronger than most men, but smarter as well. His counsel served Halberd on many difficult occasions.

But not even the wise council of Usuthu could save Halberd from Grettir.

The Pursuit of Grettir

Halberd's head cleared. The memory of his all-night battle faded. He looked around to mark his bearings. While he had been deep in reverie his body had carried him several leagues through the snow. Halberd had not felt the cold. He had not noticed the slices in his leggings nor the cuts on his lower legs, all caused by sinking through the sharp frozen crust. Halberd stopped and drank deeply from his skin flask of water. He still had some distance to go.

Usuthu lived far from the village. He preferred privacy. The Northmen preferred that Usuthu's gods stay as far from their own as possible. It was a long cold walk.

Halberd had slogged past the village, past his father's farm, and past the stone wall which marked the edge of their territory. Here the forest was thick and silent and the snow was less deep. Halberd now sank only to his ankles with each step. He did not notice the snow, did not feel the cold, did not even look up to see how far he had to go. He was lost in thought.

Like a caravan of camels led by dark-skinned

slave traders from the Land of Sand on the Inland Sea, Halberd's memories marched into his head, one after the other. Just as the endless string of laden camels are bound together, the tail of the first lashed to the neck of the second, so one thought inevitably led to another.

With the discovery of his spirit brother, Halberd had felt his life to be almost complete. The only aspect lacking was the love of a woman. There were several, in his village and other villages nearby, whom Halberd might have chosen, but his heart longed only for the one he could never have: his brother's betrothed, Grettir.

When they returned to their village Grettir was waiting. Her hair was blond and shone in the sun. Hanging free in the wind, it reached below her waist. She was tall as Halberd, with a slender neck and a sharp, defined chin. Her flashing eyes were blue-green. Her body was tight and strong, with a narrow waist, long legs, and small, high breasts.

Born of a warrior clan in another village, she had grown up with Valdane and they had assumed marriage to one another since an early age. Smart and headstrong, she spent much time with Thessah, learning all she could of the myths of the Northmen and the power of the various gods.

Though her eyes and body screamed of lust, no rumors or bad talk had ever circulated about her. Only Halberd suspected some darker side. And he was infatuated with her.

Since he had first felt the stirrings of manhood in his twelfth year she had been the object of his fantasies. He felt no jealousy for his brother. Halberd simply wanted to bed his brother's woman. Halberd was deeply ashamed of this urge, and this made him, as a young man, shy and tongue-tied around Grettir.

She provoked his shyness with darting glances or cool appraising looks when they were alone. If she passed him on the path to his parents' house she would stop him and demand he talk with her awhile. She would stand with her hands on her hips and her breasts and hips thrust toward him, chatting about her visit with Thessah. She always seemed to be daring him into some action, but Halberd never knew what it was.

When Halberd returned with Fallat's head, the attitude of the village toward him changed. He was no longer the mystical boy with the potential to lead them spiritually. He was now a man, a full-fledged shaman, and the elders looked to him for guidance. He grew into this role slowly, filling out in his body as he did in mind and spirit.

Valdane took him on raids and taught him more and more in the ways of water and war, while Thessah began confiding the secrets of the Grandmothers: the occult history of the tribe that none but the shaman could know.

As Halberd's knowledge grew, and the respect of the village increased, Grettir began to insist that she had as much right to the shaman's knowledge as he. So, Halberd was pleased to teach her what he knew. For hours they would sit in his stone house as he explained the Dream World to her. She seemed to know more than she would admit. She never told Halberd whether she journeyed there.

Halberd scarcely heard his own words to her over the beating of his heart and the blood pounding in his manhood. When the night grew dark and the lesson would go on and on, Grettir would lean forward and rest one hand on his thigh, apparently without realizing its effect. It required all of Halberd's will not to fling her to the floor.

If Valdane knew of his brother's lust for his wife he gave no sign. He encouraged her lessons with Halberd. "He will bring out your gentle side," Valdane used to say to her in Halberd's presence. "She is too much a warrior. She is not enough of a Skald like our mother."

As the time for Valdane's exploration to the West drew near, Grettir stopped her lessons with Halberd. She trained with the sword and bow instead. No one was surprised. She would be the only woman among the first shipload of explorers, and they were going to a harsh and unknown land.

Usuthu told Halberd he believed strange spirits were appearing in the village at night, spirits that only a woman could summon. Usuthu believed that Grettir knew far more than she was admitting to Halberd, but Halberd dismissed the thought.

"Perhaps she is dabbling in spells or venturing into the Dream World without being aware of it," he told Usuthu. "She is too innocent to call upon these spirits on purpose."

Valdane's wedding marked the day his ship

would sail west. His crew were brave and strong. Most were chosen from other villages. No single village would send an entire boatload on a journey this dangerous. If no one returned, who would protect the village or go on raids to increase its wealth? Danyeel had allowed only Mahvreeds, among his sons, to accompany Valdane. Mahvreeds had the most caution and common sense among all of Halberd's brothers. Danyeel thought he would protect Valdane.

With a divided heart, Halberd watched Grettir marry his brother. During the feast she approached Halberd and led him away from the village into a field. To his shock, she turned to look him in the eye and took both of his hands into hers.

"I wanted to tell you goodbye and thank you for all that you have taught me. But I must know—why have you never tried to kiss me?"

"You are my brother's wife," stammered Halberd. "I could not."

"I know that you have always loved me, as I have loved you. Your brother protects me. He does not love me as you do, with all your spirit. He cares for me and admires me, but you worship me, is this not so?"

Her eyes burned into Halberd. He took a deep breath. "Yes, it is so. But why say these things to me now, now as you are about to leave?"

"Because I would have you remember me in truth, not in fantasy. Why do you think I never approached you to consummate our love?"

"Because you were trothed to Valdane."

"Nonsense. I do what I want. I would have broken that arrangement a thousand times for you. But Valdane is firstborn. To him will come the lands and the wealth of Danyeel. You will get nothing. You will wander the sea and raid for booty. How else will you make your fortune? I chose Valdane for his power and the safety it provides. I thought it meant he would never be a sea-raider. And now, on the day of my marriage, I must go across the sea farther than any Northwoman has gone before. But I am not fearful. You and your mother have taught me well. Better than you know.

"I must sail soon. We have little time. If I must die on Vinland I'll not do so unloved. Kiss me."

She stepped into his arms and pressed her body against him. He felt her nipples through her wedding gown. Overcome, he opened his mouth and kissed her.

She pulled her head back with a mocking smile. "Come now, Halberd, do you need all that mouth for kissing? Use a smaller part of it to better purpose. Close your mouth."

Halberd did so.

Crushing herself against him once more, she leaned slightly upward and pressed her lips to his as gently as a butterfly. He felt his heart would break.

"Isn't that better?" she asked.

"Yes."

She kissed him again, as softly as a caress.

"Isn't that better?"

And again.

"Isn't that better?"

She rubbed her thighs against his and nuzzled his neck with her lips.

"Isn't that better?"

Halberd forgot his brother, forgot his village, and forgot the ways of the Northmen. He could remember only his love for Grettir. She ran her hands up his fur leggings and under his leather kilt, where his leggings ended. She took his love for her in her hands and discovered his love was strong and boutiful. With an animal cry she raised her wedding gown to her hips and pulled her husband's brother down on top of her.

They were together in the field until long after the wedding feast had ended. When at last she climbed into the dragonhead ship and waved to Halberd, the smell of his love was still upon her.

The memory of Grettir clung to him like the blood-stench of battle. Halberd remembered her soft moans in the field. But with equal clarity he recalled her mocking laugh as she stood over Valdane's body. Still his heart raced and his groin ached.

He slowed his pace until he stood still in the ankle-deep snow, the whistling wind tearing through his furs. He let the wind freeze him, not just to drive out her memory, but also as punishment. Had their illicit love driven her into madness and black sorcery? Had their lust triggered in her the desire to slay Valdane?

Valdane must have his revenge, if only to stem the overwhelming grief in Halberd's heart.

Halberd grew calm. He would not be felled by his own guilt. Lingering in his heart with all its power, it would not deter him from his journey.

Halberd gazed carefully at the snow-covered forest. He understood where he was. He had reached the path to Usuthu's yurt.

The large round tent, made of skins with the fur outward, rested on a wooden frame which kept it above the snow. Enormous wooden wheels allowed it to be moved. In the summer Halberd was never sure where Usuthu might be encamped. Once the snows fell, however, Usuthu stayed in one place.

Usuthu gave Halberd a bowl of hot, meaty soup and waited patiently for him to speak. Warmed by the soup, Halberd searched for the words.

"Grettir has returned. She visited me last night in the Dream World."

"I know," Usuthu said. "Last night Wotan warned me off her trail. She now controls him. She tried to learn the way of Bahaab Dahaabs and failed. In that failure she turned to the Evil One, Wotan. She is powerful beyond my understanding."

"Yes," Halberd replied. "In her time on Vinland she must have learned Skræling magic. No one has learned to travel in the Dream World in so little time. She has gifts which I lack. She frightens me."

"So, we must be strong."

They sat in silence as the embers in Usuthu's small cooking broiler cracked and spat.

"Usuthu, my brother, I must sail to Vinland, perhaps even to the Unknown World. The journey will be many days over the sea. I cannot ask you to face that."

"I have consulted the stars. I am prepared. When shall we depart?"

"No ship has ever crossed the Sea of Blackness during the winter months. Who will form our crew?"

"Warriors get restless. They clamor for adventure."

"Perhaps," Halberd said. "But the elders will not welcome one who would take their strong men from them in winter. We must call a council."

Danyeel sat to the right of the Village Elder. Normally he would lead this council. His son's involvement precluded that. In keeping with the tradition, Halberd had told Danyeel nothing of the cause of the meeting.

Five of the eldest and strongest leaders sat at the table in the Great Stone Hall. Thirty young warriors, among them all of Halberd's remaining brothers, sat on the floor. Halberd stood by the table with Usuthu behind him, watching from the shadows.

"My father, elders and brothers, I bring bad news. Last night Grettir visited me in the Dream World. She has slain my brother and fled to the Unknown World. Grettir has become a Skræling witch of awesome power. She bade me follow her. I will not wait until spring as planned. I will leave now. I require a crew."

Danyeel stood. His stool fell behind him and crashed to the floor.

"I take my leave to comfort my wife," he said in a broken voice. "Halberd's prophesy, which I do not question, lies heavy upon my heart. If Valdane, my eldest and bravest is slain, then Mahvreeds, who sailed with him and looked to him for counsel in all matters, cannot yet live.

"I can bear the loss of no more sons. Yet, truly, you must avenge your brother and you must have one man at your side that you may trust absolutely. Therefore, Halberd, I forbid you to take any of my sons but Labrans on your journey. A warrior's life is all he craves, and a warrior's death is his lot, no doubt. If I ordered him to stay he would go just the same, so take him.

"Good fortune to you, Halberd. Your power, which I have always encouraged you to understand, may well not be a gift, but a curse. Even if you survive the voyage I doubt I will ever see you again. Embrace me."

They met beside the table. His father hugged him tightly. While embracing, Danyeel whispered in Halberd's ear in a choked voice.

"If that witch has killed my eldest boy, then you must carve out her heart. Do not rest until vengeance is yours. Your older brothers come before you, so I cannot give you gold. Hence, you must steal it. Reach into my cloak and take the pouch."

Halberd slid his hand into his father's robe as they embraced and pulled forth a small bag. This he slid into his own robes. None in the Great Stone Hall had seen the exchange.

"Father, it will take some days to build the ship," Halberd whispered. "Will I not see you during that time?"

"No, Halberd, my heart is broken. If I saw you

I would forbid you to go to a similar fate, and that I must not do."

Danyeel released him and turned to the assembled men.

"If any man can sail the Sea of Blackness in winter," he boomed, the old strength rising in his voice, "it is Halberd. I say give him a crew and aid to build a ship. Labrans, my boy, you despise the farm and crave adventure above all things. Now you shall have it. Here is your inheritance."

Danyeel drew another pouch of coins from his robe and flung it across the room. Labrans caught it deftly, his eyes agleam with tears. He nodded gravely to his father and said nothing.

"That gold is yours, Labrans. Do not spend it to build your brother's ship. If the council refuses him, come home."

The elders took some time to recover from their shock. Valdane's expedition to Vinland was to have meant new lands to settle, new seas to plunder. A warrior of his stature, slain by a witch, by his own wife no less! It might be better to leave Vinland well enough alone. Clearly the place was cursed.

"What of the remaining crew?" argued Halberd. "They might yet be on Vinland, waiting for our aid."

"Young man, be quiet," barked Lif, the oldest man of the village. "We know what questions to ask and how to make a decision. Sit there by your friend, the black demon who serves the Giants and Dwarves, and keep your mouth shut."

Stung by these high-handed remarks, Halberd

pulled his sword from its shoulder scabbard and crashed it down upon the council table. The table split in two and fell into the laps of the elders.

"Know this, old man." Halberd spoke with the full voice of authority which is the shaman's right. "If I must hew and trim every tree with my sword to build my ship, this I shall do. My brother is dead and his murderess escapes as we debate. I will not wait for your confused heads to settle this issue. If I and Usuthu must swim the Sea of Blackness, we shall."

At these words all the young men cheered their support and crowded around Halberd, clamoring to be selected for his crew. They clanged their swords and beat the butts of their axes against the floor. Usuthu stood in the corner, watching the display impassively.

"Go then, headstrong fool!" said Lif, speaking for the council. "Take this demon from our land and good riddance. But no aid shall come to you from us. Build the ship from your own resources and the hammers of your crew. Odin frowns on fools, and this enterprise will not be blessed by him."

"Of Odin I cannot speak, Lif, but other gods I know, and they give me encouragement. When our ship is built I will invoke their names and we will see that I am right. In the meanwhile, stand in my way at your own risk."

The council was ended.

Halberd chose carefully among the young warriors. Some were chosen for caution, some daring. Here there was a fine navigator, there an archer of renown. Some would fight at the slightest provocation, others could aid with tactics. But all were brave and all were patient, a virtue that might be more important than any other during Vinland's six months of sunless winter.

Half the crew set out immediately into the forest. The ringing cries of their axes on the trees sounded even through the howling wind and blowing snow. The other ten made for the smithy to forge weapons or the grazing grounds to search for the giant elk. They would need much dried meat and even more furs and skins for winter clothing, tents, and boots.

Halberd and Usuthu met in Usuthu's stone house.

"My brother," Usuthu said, "I shall return to my yurt. Your Northmen do not wish my company on any hunt."

"And why should they?" Halberd replied. "You shoot down their elk before they even see the herd. Your horse outruns their ponies and you outride them while sleeping soundly on your horse's back."

"And," the Mongol said, "they believe that I am a demon, a servant of the Giants and Dwarves."

"Yes," Halberd answered, "and if you brought me home to live upon the Great Steppes your tribal brothers would shun me as mine shun you. It is the way of the world."

"Our preparations for this journey will not be made with hunts and building hammers," Usuthu said. "You and I must undertake a vision quest. So far as I know, two men have never pursued a vision together. Yet our fates are bound. We have no choice. I will construct a sweat-lodge and prepare the herbs we will require. There is much to ponder. Finish your earthly tasks quickly. We have a chore to share that no men but us may accomplish."

Usuthu left the stone house and made his way through the snow, the drifts barely reaching his ankles. Though nothing on earth frightened him, he knew a full measure of uncertainty. He must commune with his own gods and determine his worthiness to undertake this voyage. No Mongol traveled on the sea. Did the gods of the Great Steppes have power over the sea? Or would the gods of the Northmen, the Giants and Dwarves who held sway over the sea, rule him? What form would Bahaab Dahaabs chose to take for this journey? Usuthu would be busy.

Halberd spent his time with the boat builders. Though the Elders forbade the village to help, friends of his father trickled down to watch the keel being laid and to offer their advice. The secret of the Northman ship was its broad beam and shallow but perfectly sculpted keel. Only a master builder could lay it correctly.

Mälar, the great shipbuilder of the Northland, appeared the day the keel was to be laid.

"Word of your quest has spread, my son," he said to Halberd. "The ship you require must be slender and flexible. She must need no deep-water ports or wharfs. The keel must be oak and the beams spruce. If any ship can navigate these seas in winter, it is mine. Go to your house and seek your visions. I will build your ship."

Stunned by this generous offer, Halberd did as he was bade. For two weeks he remained in his house, praying to Thor and calling upon Heimdall, the tireless watchman who manned the gate of Aasgard. Heimdall could see an enemy approaching from around the world. Halberd would need his diligence and his acute vision.

Blizzards came through and the sky cleared. The sun circled the village for its hour or two each day and vanished. Great hunts were made and huge logs sawed. Provisions were brought aboard, new swords pounded from layers of steel, and shields cut from leather and copper. A sail was sewn and a dragonhead carved for the upcurving prow. Oars were cut from the living oak, hewn from giant slabs of wood and carved down, always made from a single piece of the tree. Three times twenty oars were made, for oars always broke. Spears were cut and shaved down for perfect straightness, and their iron heads stropped to a razor's sharpness. Baskets of arrows were cut, feathered, and armed. A giant canopy was sewn and the frame to hang it over the deck was secured to the gunwhales by wooden bolts. The oarsmen had no seats, but seachests were brought aboard and bolted to the neck by the oar holes. In these their gear would be stowed and on them they would sit to row.

Casks of water, skins of sour milk, barrels of mead, and bags filled with dried meat and salted fish and fruit were packed in the snow next to the shipbuilding site. They would stay frozen and ready until the day of departure.

From a pile of giant timbers the ship grew steadily. After the oaken keel came the spruce ribs, overlapping and curving gently upward. Once the sides were fastened, the deck was built over them. In the midst of this deck a single stump was bolted and the center carved from the stump. Into this hole the mast was set, with a giant wooden bolt run through its base as a pivot, on which the mast would be raised and lowered as wind demanded. Lines were run through the mast and the sail was attached and furled.

Shields were hung along the sides and painted black and yellow. Disks were cut and swung over the oar holes, to be swung out of the way when the oars were used and to cover the holes in heavy seas.

Mälar was as good as his word. The ship was a marvel: tight, light, seaworthy and responsive, but still powerful enough to repel attacks and the highest seas. Mälar came to Halberd's stone house with Usuthu in tow. Mälar had sailed the world many times, been to the Land of Sand to trade slaves for silver and had even sailed to the southern shore of the Island of Mountains of Fire. Usuthu was not the strangest thing Mälar had seen.

"Your ship is ready," he said, "but for the side rudder. This poses my final problem. The rudder must be designed for the man who will wield it. In this case you have no helmsman. I don't know for whom to cut it. Should it be you?"

"No," Halberd answered. "My skills lie elsewhere. Has no one come forward to guide the ship?"

"Only one man," said the shipwright. "And I do not think you want him in your crew." Behind Mälar, Usuthu smiled into his hand.

"Who is this brave soul, whose ability you doubt?" asked Halberd.

"Janor the Insane." Usuthu broke out in cackles of glee. Janor was his best friend in the village. His daft outbursts upset Mälar greatly, so that he was incapable of seeing the gift for steering that was Janor's only joy in life.

"Janor will do," Halberd said brusquely. "Cut the rudder for him alone."

The ship was finished. It rested on poles by the bay, ready to be rolled into the sea. Beside the ship, almost covered with snow, was a small round hut made of skins. Usuthu had built it while Halberd communed with the gods.

In it was a hearth of stones and a floor of dirt. The skin walls were overlapping and tight. The fire was built to great heat and stones were placed in the flames. When the stones were white-hot, water was poured onto them and the small lodge filled with steam. Halberd and Usuthu climbed inside.

"For three days we will fast and pursue our visions," Halberd told his crew. "Do not open the doors or heed our cries. When the sun rises on the third day, however, remove us quickly."

The spirit brothers climbed into the lodge, and Labrans laid the final skins over the door hole. Inside it was stiflingly hot. The steam burned their lungs with every breath. Their eyes burned and the drops stung their hands.

"Ah, my brother," gasped Halberd, "I have sailed the Northern Sea in the dead of winter and never has cold torn through me as does this heat."

His chest heaved as he fought for a breath in the moist, searing air.

"Indeed," he continued, "I've sailed the Inland Sea when no man could pull an oar, so fierce was the sun, yet I could still draw a breath. Here I feel that I will drown while on solid land."

"Quiet, Halberd. Be still in your mind and value patience," Usuthu said gently. "These first moments are the worst. Soon you will be calm, and after that, what your body feels will not matter. Chant your spells and waste no more breath in speech. I shall not be able to hear you, but know that I am by your side."

And so they sat in silence, each pursuing his own spells. After a few hours the steam dissipated. They felt clean and purified. They slept.

In the black lodge there was neither night nor day. Time meant nothing. Both sat on the floor, each listening only to his own breathing and heartbeat.

Suddenly the floor gave way under Halberd. He was plummeting, falling down through an endless blue sky. From above he gazed down on a peaceful landscape. An undulating river ran through a green forest. Resting on the banks of the river were long, narrow boats of a type he had never seen. Dark-haired people dressed in soft animal skins lived next to the river in strange pointed skin houses with poles protruding from the top. The faces of this tribe resembled Usuthu's people, but the eyes were not as slanted nor the cheeks as broad. They were taller and less squat in build than the Mongols. Their skin was reddish-brown rather than yellow.

As he hovered in the clear blue sky above these people, he became aware of a presence filling the sky around him. Floating like a cloud, he rolled slowly over onto his back and gazed into the blue heavens. Above him, outlined but not quite visible, was a beautiful face. It was a lovely young woman with flowing black hair framing a gentle, beckoning face. Though the sky was blue above him the face was obscured somehow, as if clear clouds were drifting across it. She smiled at Halberd with great warmth and love. A feeling of peace and contentment ran through him. He longed to get closer to her, to touch her. He reached his hand up toward her. As he did so, she vanished.

Halberd awoke to the shouts of his crew as they dragged the skins from the entrance. He was lying on the damp floor of the sweat lodge, exhausted and hungry. His head pounded. Next to him, his face set hard as nails, sat Usuthu.

"Hold!" Halberd shouted to his crew. "Leave the skins in place. Give us peace for a few moments more."

The crew withdrew.

Halberd leaned to Usuthu. "Tell me, brother, what did you see?"

"Giant serpents assaulted us in the Great Open Ocean," Usuthu began. "We sailed through waves higher than the mast and black as night. Dragons snatched our crew from the deck and dragged them into the raging sea. When we were free of the dragons the Giant Nidhogg attacked us without mercy. I do not even know this Giant or these gods, yet I see them in my visions. Lizards rose from the ocean floor and in their eyes I saw Grettir, alive and with flaming hair."

Usuthu seldom showed emotion. Now he was worried. "When our ship faces these dangers I will be bound to the mast. There is no other way for me. Who among our crew can aid you in fighting off Nidhogg? Why do I see these things in my visions? Never have I asked another for council concerning my own quest. Bahaab Dahaabs guides me, but now I am drifting. Have I lost contact with the gods of my people?"

"You have these visions because our voyage is filled with danger," Halberd answered. "We will encounter spirits in the Open Ocean no mortal has seen. The gods are telling you what to expect. Myself, I dreamed of a peaceful, green land and a beautiful young woman. I think both peace and violence await us."

"Perhaps. You must delay the launch by one more day. I will remain in this lodge and create Bahaab Dahaabs in the image he requires."

When Halberd emerged from the sweat lodge he glanced at his sword, which leaned against the door. The Jewel of Kyrwyn-Coyne blazed like the brighest star in the heavens. Lif and the elders were waiting. "What did you see?" Lif demanded.

"I saw a young woman who called to me with great love. I will sail to find her."

"And who will pay for the labor these men have done?"

Mälar stepped forward. "I will take no pay for my services," he said. "Except to be allowed to sail in the Great Open Ocean."

Halberd smiled. "You are welcome to sail with us, Mälar."

Halberd pulled the pouch containing his inheritance from his robe and counted out half the coins in it to Lif. "One quarter of these coins are for the craftsmen who are not in my crew," he said. "And the other three quarters are for any of my crew who return alive. I commend these coins to you for safekeeping."

Lif nodded gravely.

"And this," Halberd said, pulling a small silver piece from the pouch, "is for the new council table." As the villagers standing behind Lif began to howl with laughter, Halberd turned to his crew.

"Load our ship."

They formed a line and passed the provisions on board, each man stowing what he needed in his chest. The weapons went into a central chest and the food was divided out and each man put his portion away. Water and giant casks of mead were secured to the deck and oars were slid into racks along the gunwale.

Usuthu came through the snow, clad in his shields and conical helmet, towering over the Northmen. He carried only his longbow and a quiver of arrows and a tiny carved Northman.

"What is that totem?" Lif demanded.

"If is the chieftain of all my gods, Bahaab

Dahaabs. He has commanded me to carve his likeness as that of the tribe in which I have been adopted. And so I have."

"What did he say?" Lif asked of Halberd. Usuthu had spoken, as always, in the language of the Steppes.

"He said it was time to be off," replied Halberd.

His crew leaned their shoulders to the slender ship, and she slid down her bed of poles and into the bay, cracking the thin coat of ice that formed on its surface overnight. The men cheered and swung a gangplank to the ship's gunwale. One by one they climbed aboard. When they were all in place Usuthu gingerly walked up the plank and sat down in front of the mast. His tiny god he placed on the deck before him.

Halberd mounted the deck and nodded at Janor the Insane. He put the rudder into water for the first time. Halberd felt the decks beneath his feet. The ship seemed solid and light at the same time; air and water, fire and ice all mixed together. She was a charmed vessel.

Mälar called from his post beside Janor: "What is the name of this hardy ship?"

"The *Freyja,*" spake Halberd, and a short silence followed.

"Odin's wife, a good name," said Mälar. "The Giants and Dwarves of the sea lust for her just as she protects us from them. She is as beautiful as the goddess herself. She is strong, and, I hope, as cunning as her namesake."

Halberd looked no more at his village or the other ships on shore beside the bay. He turned his eyes to the west and nodded at Janor.

Janor dipped the steering rudder into the thin skin of ice that covered the bay, and the ice cracked. The rudder tasted the water for the first time.

"Oars!" cried Mälar, and every crewman drew his oar from its holder and ran it out its hole.

"Stroke!" sounded Mälar, and the ice on the bay crunched as twenty oars bit into the bay.

Halberd walked to the bow as the ship began to move. He leaned onto one leg and rested his hand on the curved dragonhead which surmounted the prow.

"Stroke!" came the cry, and the ship shot forward, crashing through the thin ice and heading into the western current.

The *Freyja* skimmed over the bay like a bird. Ice flew every time the oars dipped, and the village swiftly fell from sight. Soon they were in open water and the sail was raised. The *Freyja* plunged from crest to crest like a happy horse. She was a seagoing delight, a ship to take pride in.

As land fell behind them Halberd did not look back. Behind lay only his village, now lost forever, and the memories of the betrayal of his brother. Before him was Grettir, his revenge and absolution.

The Open Sea

Once clear of the bay the *Freyja* seemed to steer herself. The oars were shipped and the wind remained strong. Janor the Insane was quiet and alert. He never left the helm. Mälar slept on deck beside the helmsman on the first night.

The sea was light. Usuthu's terror slackened enough for him to sit on deck, with merely a bit of cord around his waist to hold him to the mast. Halberd never left his post at the bow. He stared west, into the night, trying to see the dangers which lay ahead.

The great landmass of the Northland fell behind them to the north and east. By the middle of the first night, when the stars were brightest, the *Freyja* cleared all sight of land. The smell of the ocean changed. It became cleaner, wilder, and more dangerous. The land and forest gods held no power here. The Giants and Dwarves ran the sea, and they were a capricious lot. No one in the Known World, however, knew these wild gods better than the Northmen.

Dawn never came on the second day. No sun shone and the moon did not set. A dense fog had descended. Janor, standing by the rudder, could not discern Halberd as he rested one hand on the prow. The men spoke in whispers and kept one hand on their swords. It was not an auspicious way to begin a journey.

Oddly, though the fog was thick, the breeze was fresh. They were not becalmed. In fact, they raced through the fog as they had through the clear night, cutting through or leaping over the waves. But these waves they could barely see. Janor shoved Mälar forward to find Halberd. Mälar, experienced on water like none aboard the vessel but Janor, was still frightened by the fog and did not want to move. The other crewmen remained on their chests, one hand on their swords, waiting for a sea Dwarf to reach from the fog and snatch them to the bottom of the sea.

Mälar stumbled the length of the ship, tripping over one of Usuthu's vast legs. Usuthu sat against the mast, sleeping deeply. When Mälar struck his leg he awoke with a start.

"Leave me be, old man," he shouted. "When I cannot see the water I am unafraid. I must sleep as long as this cloud surrounds us, for I will not when it is gone."

"What did he say?" Mälar asked Halberd, who had come to the mast when Usuthu began shouting.

"He said to let him sleep. What is our course?"

"Janor cannot say. Nor can I. Fog such as this is new to both of us. We would ship the sail and wait for it to pass."

"No," said Halberd vehemently. "The wind blows hard but the fog does not lift. Either it extends for many leagues or is demonically sent. Either way we will waste days we may not spare.

Let the winds take us. They blow mainly to the west."

"If they blow wrong," Mälar said, "we may end upon the rocks of the Heathland Isles. Or worse yet, in the hands of the Heathmen."

"So be it. As long as this fog holds, relieve Janor from the rudder. There is no course to hold. Let him sleep while he may."

And so for three days and nights they raced on through the fog. The grayness never lightened nor grew thicker. The wind never slackened but it could not blow the fog away. Either the whole Northern Sea was shrouded in gray or the *Freyja* traveled in her own tiny cloud. Either way, the ship was not happy.

The dampness of the fog soaked everything, including the food and the bedrolls. With no day or night the crew could not sleep comfortably. They awoke to no light and went to sleep in no darkness. The sea seemed fairly calm, but steering through the limitless gray made whoever manned the helm uneasy. Rocks grew in the imagination until whole islands seemed ready to rear up and smash the boat to kindling.

The fog clung to the surface of the ocean and blotted out the sea. It crept through the oar holes and coiled around the feet of the sleeping crewmen. The sail, full of wind and only a few feet above the deck, was invisible.

Usuthu simply slept. As long as he could not see the water he was relaxed. He did not awaken again, nor did he seem to require food or water. He appeared to be storing strength. The tiny image of Bahaab Dahaabs remained clutched in his hand.

Halberd took his time at the helm and tried to rest, but the fog unnerved him as well. Was Grettir's power so great that she could send this fog from halfway across the world? The crew spoke to him in hushed voices, asking him when it would lift and where they would be when it did. Most believed that they had been killed and were now being born away to Niflheim, the Land of the Dead, which was guarded by the Giant Nidhogg.

Halberd countered this superstition by telling all who believed they were dead to refrain from eating. By the morning of the third day they were hungry enough to accept that they still lived. This good news did not allay their fears.

Late into the third night or early into the third morning, the fog simply vanished. It did not melt away or gradually disperse. One moment it surrounded them, gray and dripping, the next the sky was clear. The wind remained fresh. It was near dawn.

Janor could read their fate with one glance at the stars. He stared for a moment and began to cackle. Mälar studied the sky and said nothing. He walked to the weapon chest amidships and removed his bow. Sitting down to string it, he looked to the southern horizon and prayed in a soft voice to the god of war, the lord of Aasgard, Odin. Clearly Odin had brought them here because he demanded a sacrifice in blood from any Northman so audacious as to dare the Open Ocean in winter.

Kirstin, young and brave, but inexperienced, went to the prow.

"Halberd," he asked, "where are we? What do the stars tell?"

"Their message is simple, Kirstin. We have been blown far south of our intended course. South and west of us by less than a day lie the Heathland Isles. When we are in sight of land the Heathmen will no doubt attack us. First we must clear the Heathland landfall, which is never easy. Once past that we must run through the scattered isles. In those straits are many settlements which guard the richest monasteries. We have sacked them many times. They are alert and fiendish. When they see us we must fight for our lives."

"Is it true they eat the flesh of their captives?"

"Yes," Halberd said. "Now prepare your bow."

As dawn broke red and clear the Northmen all knew where they were. Most of them had been here on raids in earlier times, but that had been deliberate. Their ships had been provisioned for attack and a quick return to their own land. Today they had thousands of leagues yet to sail. A prolonged battle now might weight them down with casualties or deplete their stock of arrows or even cripple the journey itself.

To the west rose the craggy dark landfall of Heathland. The waves crashed into the broken rocks and spewed foam hundreds of feet up the ragged cliffs. Atop the highest northernmost point of land was a bleak fortress. Accessible only by a shallow bay and a treacherous climb up the slick cliffs, it was considered the most protected monastery in Heathland. Considered thus until Valdane and his crew had sacked it some years ago. The Heathmen had not thought it possible for a warship to land in so shallow a harbor. They were wrong.

Since that attack they had burned for revenge against the Northmen. Any dragonships in their waters were sunk and the crews eaten. The savage Heathmen were protected-waters sailors and, in their own territory, feared pirates. Halberd had hoped to avoid them but the fog had decided otherwise.

Janor fought the rudder as the current tried to fling them up against the vast landfall. He cried for Usuthu to help hold the rudder with his great strength, but Usuthu refused to budge. Halberd had bound him to the mast from the waist down, leaving his arms free to wield his bow.

Labrans left his chest to stand by Janor. Together they wrapped their arms around the giant rudder and pulled with all their might. Crewmen leaned into the lines that controlled the sail, grappling against the wind to pull the ship clear of the foamy crags. Mälar gripped the gunwale and called the course. Labrans and Janor pulled the rudder to his command.

The wind tried to pull the *Freyja* onto the rocks, but the crew was stronger than the wind. Northmen ships were built to sail the sea, not be vanquished by it, and the *Freyja* was a special ship. Bit by bit Janor and Labrans steered the ship clear of the broken, knifelike rocks. They passed by near enough to feel the spray rebound off the cliffs. As the sea dashed itself onto the jagged stones, themselves as big as three ships put together, the white brine spewed over the men like a deadly rain.

Any oars out on the south side of the *Freyja* would have been crushed against the rocks, so close did the ship pass. The crewmen held their breath as the ship slid by. Usuthu could only stare, his mouth hanging open, his great arms slack at his side.

Halberd stayed at the prow, clinging to the curving neck of the dragonhead prow as to the mane of a runaway pony. The dancing bow tried to toss him into the spume, but he held on with all his strength as the rocks swept by.

Once they were clear of the landfall the wind sharpened. The *Freyja* surged forward, leaving the deadly cliffs behind her. The sun climbed into its chariot and soared into the sky. The black rocks turned red from the dawn, and the white spray shone gold. Even Mälar turned his eyes from the sea ahead, awestruck at the change in the cliffs which had swallowed so many other boats.

The crew lifted their heads from their oars and cheered with relief. Their arms never stopped working.

"Save your breath!" shouted Mälar. "One danger is passed but another looms."

Halberd turned at these words, tearing his eyes from the shining cliffs.

"What threatens us now, Mälar?" he called. "Have we not escaped the cliffs?"

"The cliffs, aye, but not the cliff-dwellers. Behold!"

Mälar pointed his bony hand toward the blood-red cliff-tops. Atop the monastery walls tiny figures waved torches in large arcs. The flames twirled in the twilight.

"What means those flames, Mälar?" asked Kirstin. His question was grunted out between hard-earned breaths as he lashed his oar through the racing sea.

Halberd was not the only man who did not bother to turn back to hear Mälar's reply. Those who were familiar with the strait knew all too well the answer.

"Those cursed monks," said Mälar, "signal to their protectors, the cannibal Heathmen. At every isle we pass flames will glow. By these fires the Heathmen will mark our progress. Before we see the open ocean we will battle for our lives."

"And our flesh," spake Janor with a cackle.

"What does the insane one mean by this?" cried Kirsten.

"He means," replied Mälar, "that if we fight well we shall yet dine upon another meal and if we fight poorly . . ."

"We shall become one," interrupted Janor. "That is what I mean."

Kirstin dropped his head and pulled at his oar. His thoughts and his fears were his own private matter. No man but Janor would dare tease about so dire a subject.

Beyond the landfall the course was straightforward. Lying between the landfall and the Sea of Blackness were the scattered Heathland Isles, tiny ragged islands of wind-scoured scrub plants and settlements of lightless granite homes. The Heathmen burned the earth in lieu of firewood. Every scrap of wood that washed shore they used to build their ships. In winter, like all people of the sea, they hunkered down for the long nights and short days.

If they were shocked to find a dragonship of Northmen in this wild sea during these cold months they did not show it by sloth in preparation for battle. As the *Freyja* sailed through the first of the straits they saw the waving torches at every promontory. The signal was passing from island to island, and at one of them would be waiting a battle fleet.

The crew prepared their arrows and lances. Swords would not be important. Given the numbers of Heathmen that opposed them, if the *Freyja* was boarded and the fighting became hand-to-hand, all was lost. Small iron braziers were filled with coals, lit, and set up about the ship. In these would be dipped the heads of the fire-arrows, which were wrapped with cloth and pitch. Once alight, they would be sent against the Heathmen ships. Unlike the Northmen, the men of the Heathland Isles sealed their ships with pitch. If struck properly, their ships would burn like cordwood.

The crew knelt below the level of the gunwale, protected by the yellow-and-black shields that hung over the sides of the ship. Island by tiny island they sailed their way through the straits. At every settlement they saw the waving torches, but no ships. The sun moved through the sky and the night stars appeared. The wind never slacked and the *Freyja* moved westward.

There was little threat of an attack at night. Clearly the Heathmen were gathering their forces and would strike at the Channel of Death, the final and most narrow strait before the Sea of Blackness. Halberd commanded Janor to rest. Halberd would need the insane one's skills during the battle. Halberd likewise sent Mälar from the helm. Though the night dragged few of the other Northmen could sleep.

They huddled around the iron braziers, the orange light reflecting off their grave faces. They tested their bows and sighted down their arrows, choosing the straightest ones. All prayed for the night to end and the fight to be joined. None were cowards and all knew the wait was worse than the bloodshed.

Halberd stayed near Usuthu at the mast, taking counsel. They had not yet been in battle together, though they had gone on many hunts.

"The only good aspect of this is the speed of the wind," Halberd explained. "Despite the narrowness of the channel they will have a limited time in which to attack. They will not follow us into the Sea of Blackness. I believe we can outrun them in this wind and outmaneuver any blockade."

Usuthu seemed deep in thought. "What are their strategies?" he asked.

"They have none. They like to swarm. They fight like devils and seem to feel no pain. Wounds do not deter them. They will fight until they die. They do not worship our gods and they deeply fear any spirits."

Usuthu grunted and said nothing more. He gripped his figure of Bahaab Dahaabs and stared far ahead, past the rushing waves and blowing spray. He seemed to look halfway around the Known World, until he could see his people riding across the Great Steppes, sweeping their enemies before them. After a long silence, he looked down at Halberd.

"My brother," he said, "I have not left the Steppes to be eaten by savages. Let them come."

With that, he leaned his huge head back against the mast and fell instantly asleep. Halberd returned to the prow. The night wore on.

The sky grew slowly red once again. The sun bounced off the steep islands and lit the surface of the roiling water as dark red as wine. Far ahead, at least half a day's sail, the Northmen could see the open water of the Sea of Blackness. Between them and this gate to the Great Open Ocean lay the narrow Channel of Death. There was no other route to or from the Sea of Blackness. Those who could navigated far to the north, to avoid the Heathmen altogether. Those who could not ran the gauntlet or perished.

The *Freyja* swept into the channel. Funneled by the islands on either side, the wind increased in force. The ship raced by the stone settlements, the forbidding cliffs, the empty stone wharfs. Here the channel was perhaps ten ship lengths wide, enough room only to fight.

Kirstin, the sharpest-eyed among the crew, pointed toward the end of the channel and cried out. In an instant the crew was on their feet. At the distant end of the channel, lying between them and the relative safety of the Sea of Blackness, stood six Heathmen ships, tossing in the wind and swells.

All the Northmen could do was wait. Wait for the wind to carry them into the teeth of their enemy. Wait for the battle to begin. Wait to see if they lived or were carried to the courts of Aasgard, there to be fêted by the maidens and even the gods themselves.

"Go and awaken Janor," commanded Halberd. "And bring Mälar to the bow. He must call the course during the fight."

The ships of the Heathmen were near enough to be seen clearly. Broad-beamed and sluggish, they were designed for pulling large fish nets or for manning blockades. Turned across the sea and anchored, as they were now, they proved stable platforms for the archers of the Heathmen.

Halberd called his crew together at the prow.

"When their first arrow flies, respond in a volley. Aim at the middle ship first, then swing outward right and left depending on the side of the ship on which you are stationed. We must burn as many as possible before we close the distance. I estimate we are still three times the distance they can shoot."

As he spoke a loud whoosh whistled over their heads. The crew turned as one, staring in astonishment and fear at the Heathmen ships. Had they fired an arrow? Why would they waste their precious weapons at so great a range? Amazingly, the middle ship of the Heathman fleet was already ablaze. She had been struck dead center by a flaming bolt.

The whoosh sounded again. The crew in the prow swung their heads sternward. Tied to the mast from the waist down, Usuthu stood relaxed, his arrow-hand releasing smoothly. The flaming arrow from his great longbow sailed in a fine arc across the afternoon sky. Soaring until it was indistinguishable against the sky, the arrow bit into another Heathmen craft. The ship was so far away the Northmen could verify the strike only when a new flower of flame blossomed from the ship.

No one spoke. Usuthu plucked another arrow from his quiver and stretched his huge arm forward. The arrow was longer than any bow belonging to the Northmen. He nocked the great shaft. He dipped the arrow into the brazier at his feet and it burst into flame. Effortlessly drawing back the string that no man in the village could even move, he raised the bow toward the heavens and let the burning shaft fly.

Again every man on board swiveled his head forward and saw another fireball erupt. Though too far away to clearly discern their faces, the Northmen could see the Heathmen were panicked. They ran to and fro on their boats, splashing water onto the flames, which had now grown too large to control. The icy water would kill in minutes, but it was a death much preferred to being roasted alive. The Heathmen leaped from their flaming ships into the dark, killing channel.

As the *Freyja* grew nearer, the Heathmen began to fire their own arrows in desperation. Their shafts did not reach even halfway to the onrushing Northmen. Usuthu calmly nocked his arrows, lit them, and let them fly. One by one the Heathmen's ships exploded into flame.

When only one remained untouched the *Freyja* was in arrow range. The Vikings let go with a concentrated volley that passed in midair the flight of flaming darts sent by the surviving Heathmen. "Now!" screamed Mälar, kneeling on the prow. In instant response Janor the Insane, with all the cunning his condition granted him, swung the great rudder outward as far as it would go.

Any other ship would have capsized. But the *Freyja* was built for dangerous maneuvers, and she turned her side to the onrushing flight and whipped away from the danger like a deer avoiding a panther's leap. The arrows fell into the sea with a sizzling plop as the Heathmen's last vessel flamed from stem to stern.

Regaining the prow, Janor drove the *Freyja* straight for the smoldering wreckage of the first ship Usuthu had hit. It was now burned to the waterline. The dragonprow struck this barge of blackened spars with a crash that sent everyone but Janor and Usuthu sprawling to the deck. The ruins of the warship crumbled into charcoal and the *Freyja* crushed through her charred remains. Bobbing in the sea were the roasted bodies of the Heathmen. Oars, broken weapons, and tatters of sails floated beside them.

A brief cloud engulfed the *Freyja* with the stench of burning flesh. Then the wind was fresh and clean. The setting sun showed the smooth sea ahead.

They had cleared the Channel of Death. They were now in the Sea of Blackness.

Beyond Heathland, there was only ocean. The

Sea of Blackness, a common raiding route during the warm months, when sane men went to sea, now was aroam with demons. Creatures from Niflheim, the Land of the Dead, were set free in winter and they ran amuck in the Sea of Blackness. Huge storms and sleet squalls came down from the Top of the World, and few men had seen them and lived to describe the bitter, sodden cold.

Usuthu saw the huge swells waiting for them as they sailed beyond the broiled flesh of their enemies. They rolled across the bows and broke across the dragonhead prow, soaking the ship from bow to stern. Usuthu was now beside himself with fear. Clutching Bahaab Dahaabs so tightly the skin over his knuckles cracked and bled, he called for Halberd.

"My brother, why is the water so large? Are the gods angry at the death of the Heathmen?"

"Before we were sailing in line with the wind and the swells were flattened before us. Now we must reach across the wind to achieve our destination. The waves will be much bigger. Also, we are now beyond all protection of land. The wind will be fierce. I think us lucky to find the seas only as large as this. They will grow huge before we reach Vinland."

"Then bind me tightly, for this I cannot abide."

Halberd called two of the crew. They carefully fastened Usuthu's weapons bag to the deck by his feet. Then they bound his chest to the mast, leaving only his arms free. The waves soaked him with every leap of the ship.

No one commented on his fear. Every warrior

fears something. If he does not he is mad. Usuthu had saved them by his destruction of the Heathmen. If the sea frightened him at least it did not affect his aim. Men had to fight on shipboard for years to understand the precise moment when to let fly an arrow at another ship. Usuthu seemed to know instinctively. Only a demon could shoot like that, but no demon would ever show fear to a mortal. So, Usuthu must be a man.

Halberd, exhausted, curled into his sleeping furs behind the seachest of his brother. Labrans took the watch by the prow. The chest offered Halberd some protection from the spray as the *Freyja* sank into every trough and burst through every crest. The swells were higher than her mast and showed no sign of dwindling. The temperature was dropping. A storm was due. Warm and dry for the moment, Halberd slept.

Lying in a flowery meadow, Halberd caresses Grettir's soft skin. She murmurs into his ear hungrily and climbs astride him. She removes his shirt and lowers her gentle lips to his nipples. As she licks them softly he groans and shifts position, the better to enter her tight softness. As he lifts her by her slender hips he sees Valdane on the crest of the meadow, watching. Shocked and instantly aware of the curse he has created, Halberd flings Grettir to the ground. As she strikes the earth she becomes a huge serpent, either Nidhogg or one of his servants. She rises to her full height, her long forked tongue flicking in and out and her sharp fangs gleaming. She strikes at Halberd. He springs to the side and from far away hears the sounds of screams.

Halberd awoke with a start, thrashing in his furs to find his sword. Something gripped his shoulder like iron, while all around him rose the cries of his crew. Labrans' face loomed above him.

"To arms, brother," shouted Labrans as he shook Halberd awake. "A dragon attacks!"

Halberd kicked his legs free of his sleeping furs. He grabbed his sword from its scabbard. Nestled in its silver web on the broadsword's hilt, the Jewel of Krywyn-Coyne glowed white-hot. As Labrans hauled Halberd to his feet, Mälar ran past, an arrow already nocked in his bow.

Half the men had left their oars. They lined the leeward gunwale, spears ready for throwing and swords raised to slash. All gazed upward with a mixture of dread, awe and, among the bravest warriors, unmistakable anticipation. Halberd stood, rooted to the deck with shock.

Rising high above the swells was the serpent from his dream. Green and showering seawater from its scales, the demon uncoiled and peered down at the ship. Its eyes were flame, pure flame. Its fangs were longer than the mast and almost as broad.

Usuthu stared into the eyes of the monster and howled into his face, confident of his magic and fearful no more.

"Vile beast," Usuthu commanded, "evil spawn of Wotan, Bahaab Dahaabs commands you, through his servant, to disperse. Leave this vessel and fall back into the sea. You are not real and no man can you injure! I, Usuthu, prince of the Great Steppes, command you to die and vanish. In the name of Nghee, I am your master!"

The snake ignored him and studied the crew and the ship with great care and cunning, as if commending them to memory. Usuthu closed his mouth and looked back with equal care. The serpent was not attacking nor retreating, but waiting for something.

While Janor and Mälar tended the helm, the crew lined the rail and hurled spears and shot arrows at the serpent. These passed right through and fell harmlessly into the heaving sea. Finally free of his furs, Halberd drew his sword and called to his crew.

"It is an apparition! Do not waste your arrows!"

At the sound of his voice the serpent turned its giant head and spotted Halberd. Instantly, it struck. As the scaly head flashed through the blowing spray, Halberd braced his feet against the rolling motion of the ship and swung with all his strength. His broadsword passed through the neck of the beast even as its great tooth caught his arm and, dragging along its length, drew a gout of blood.

As Halberd fell back on the deck clutching his wounded arm he could plainly see, in the eyes of the demon, the laughing face of Grettir. Having drawn blood, the seadragon vanished.

The seas increased in force and the wind began to howl. Janor and Mälar lashed themselves to the rudder and Halberd ordered the crew to tie themselves to their chests. He then made his way across the slick deck to confer with Usuthu.

Usuthu bound Halberd's arm. He then inclined his head to draw Halberd nearer.

"Who sent this demon? Are your gods so powerful? My spells had no effect. Further, I believe I saw the face of Grettir in the serpent's eyes."

"You did," replied Halberd. "Her power is beyond anything I have seen or been taught. The Skrælings must be as powerful as the Great-Grandfathers claimed. Surely she learned from them during her months on Vinland."

"Who are the Skrælings?"

"The natives of Vinland. The Great-Grandfathers who first saw Vinland in passing told us of them through the centuries. Valdane hoped to treaty with them and establish settlements on Vinland. Perhaps they do not exist. But something has granted Grettir power which insults our gods."

"Is it possible she is now dead, and haunts us in spirit form?"

Ice was forming in Usuthu's mustache, and he had to wipe the frozen spray from his eyelids in order to see Halberd. He asked his question without fear. If she was dead, and attacking them from the Spirit World, then different strategies would have to be employed.

"I think not," Halberd answered. "I believe I would feel her death in my dreams, or in a lightening of the curse which my disloyalty has created. When she dies I will know it. I will know it because she will lie at my feet and I will cut out her heart for my father." Halberd looked away for a moment. He shook his head to cast out his dark thoughts and continued.

"Now the storm is freshening. Let me bring you a cloak."

"No, my brother. I do not feel the cold. Tend to your tasks during this storm."

The stars were gone. In their place were gray, iron-hard clouds, low to the ship and scudding by on the shrieking wind. Snow and sleet blew sideways. The sail, though stiff with ice, still puffed out from the wind. The course was held. The crew huddled on their storage chests, chewing on their rations and keeping their heads down. Every so often they would shake the ice from their laps or crack the quickly forming sheets from around their eyes. Otherwise, they simply hung on.

Icy swells were crashing over the ship, which porpoised through each one, her bow rising high in the air, the whole ship shaking along her length and smashing into the troughs. The decks were sheathed in ice. Janor and Mälar held to the tiller for dear life, driving the ship steadily forward. A sheen of ice slowly formed over Usuthu. His lower body was encased. The ropes that bound him were frozen fast to his leggings and the mast.

Halberd, clinging to a lifeline in the prow, peered through the icy brine, struggling to see their way. He knew Grettir was a fullborn witch and temptress. Would he have the strength to face her after a journey of this difficulty?

The storm raged throughout the night. With the limp gray dawn the winds lowered a bit and the snow ceased. The crew slowly roused themselves and began to break the ice on the deck and the rigging. Though they were accustomed to miserable weather, few had spent a night exposed in such a storm. Their spirits were low and their mood as leaden as the sky.

Einar, a tough warrior of few words, came to Halberd at the prow.

"What was the demon that appeared yesterday? Whence did it come?" he asked.

"It came from the witch Grettir, the wife of my brother. She commanded it from far away."

Einar hesitated, looking at the deck and chewing on his ice-rimed beard.

"Speak," commanded Halberd. "Speak or go back to your post."

"We have a question of great gravity, that only a shaman may answer. But we fear you do not want to address this question."

Halberd was baffled. "What question might this be?"

Einar could not meet Halberd's gaze as he mumbled the question into his beard. He spoke in a whisper. "How do we know your friend, the black demon, did not summon the serpent?"

Halberd, too shocked to feel anger, knew full well how such a suspicion could wreck the voyage. "Whence," he demanded, "comes this notion?"

"Halberd," Einar whispered urgently, looking over his shoulder to ensure Usuthu did not hear, "we cannot understand him when he speaks. He called to the demon and after he did so it struck at you. How do we know he did not order it to kill you?"

"Einar," Halberd said, as if talking to a child, "Usuthu saved us from the Heathmen. Why would he do that if he wanted us dead?"

"Perhaps he serves the sea. Perhaps he is a great sailor and feigns this fear so we will not see his skills. How could a warrior as powerful as he fear the sea, which is all around us all our lives?"

"He didn't live his life near the sea, you fool! You are as afraid of Usuthu's horse as he is of the sea, and for good reason. He is my brother, and anyone who fights him is my enemy as well. Mark that, Einar. You are a brave warrior and I need your sword to fight the Skrælings, but I will pitch you into the sea to protect Usuthu."

Halberd and Einar gazed at one another, stunned. Halberd could scarcely believe his own words. He had grown up with Einar, raided with him all his life and eaten at his father's table many times. Einar seemed defeated by the rage and authority of his childhood friend. He turned slightly to avoid another blast of frigid seawater.

"I came on this adventure to serve you, Halberd, and serve I will, with all the loyalty of my oath. Fear me not, but be sure that others at the oars do not trust your giant as you do."

He turned his back on Halberd, his broad shoulders bent, his head downcast.

"Einar, I mean you no disrespect. I feel for you as I do a brother."

"No, you do not. But how could you? You are a shaman and the leader of this voyage. You must bear this responsibility, despite your youth. I forgive your harshness to an old friend." Einar now smiled. "If others resent your giant, I will defend you."

Einar turned to the lee gunwale and rested his arms. Halberd looked to the south with him. More low clouds raced toward them. As they stared at the rough seas and rolled with the plunging of the *Freyja*, the sea surged upward right before them. A huge wave swept over them, soaking through their furs and knocking them flat. Einar landed hard on the icy boards and instantly slid the length of the ship. Halberd, caught by his lifeline, reached for him in vain. Einar shot past Usuthu, who, bound to the mast, could not move. Janor dared not leave the rudder. Mälar dropped to his knees to block Einar, but another great crest knocked Mälar aside. Einar was washed over the rail and vanished from sight.

Halberd looked in horror at the huge wave. In its center rose yet another dragon, flame in its eyes and ice hanging from its fangs. Halberd peered upward, trying to discern if this monster was real or fantastic. The crew, roused by Einar's shouts as he slid to his icy grave, raised their weary heads to see the dragon above them once more.

Asvald, a farmboy from a village on the eastern shore, studied the dragon with care.

"Do not worry, my brothers," he called from his oar, "this beast cannot harm us. It, too, is merely an apparition."

Jadri, his best friend and oar-mate, nodded in agreement.

"Aye, ignore it and let us turn to and pray for our lost warrior, Einar," he said.

The dragon had waited long enough. It struck the ship. Every shield on the port side shattered. A gaping hole appeared above the gunwale. Asvald, sitting next to the gunwale, followed Einar through this hole into the frigid depths. Water rushed in over the ruined gunwale.

"Asvald, take my hand!" Jadri screamed. But Asvald was already gone.

Jadri's next words were drowned by another black wave pouring through the shattered shields. When the wave receded, Jadri had vanished.

The dragon backed off, boards hanging from its mouth.

Halberd slashed his own lifeline with his dagger while calling to his brother.

"Labrans, cut Usuthu free," he shouted. "Janor, hold the course."

The crew drew their bows once more, but discovered their arrows and strings were coated with ice. They cursed the gods and furiously wiped at their weapons. Gripping the icy gunwale, Halberd made his way amidships. Labrans rested on his knees, his battleax above his head. He was trying to cut the ropes which bound Usuthu. He slid to and fro on the icy deck. The ship reared and plunged. Under the ropes were Usuthu's legs. It was a dire moment.

"Here, brother," said Halberd. He drew his dagger and sawed at the frozen ropes. His crew lined the rail. They threw spears and shouted to ward off the dragon. It withdrew slightly and gazed quizzically at the commotion it had wrought. This beast was not Nidhogg, Giant of the sea. It was insufficiently cunning. It was but one of many dragons in the Sea of Blackness, no more, no less. Still, it could destroy the ship.

The beast circled the ship underwater and struck on the opposite side. Labrans was tossed across the deck by the force of the blow and caught only by the quick hands of the crew. The gunwale was crushed to splinters. The dragon seemed to be gauging the strength of the wooden beast it had discovered in midocean. With careful deliberation, the monster struck, almost daintily despite its bulk. Thormod, an oarsman of prodigious strength and long black hair, was carried off the ship in the serpent's mouth. He screamed for aid until the giant fangs ran him through.

Of the frozen ropes which bound Usuthu only strands remained when he wrenched his legs free. Usuthu stepped toward the beast and fell over onto his face. His frozen legs could not adjust to the movement of the wildly tossing ship.

"My lance!" he called.

Halberd tore the lance free from the weapon bag lashed to the mast. He slid the great spear to Usuthu, who lay on his stomach on the icy deck, clinging to a flapping lifeline. Usuthu snatched his lance as it bounced along the deck. He flipped onto his back and sat up quickly, one fist wrapped in the lifeline. The other held his monstrous spear.

"I am slain," cried Thormod through the bright red blood that ran between his teeth and spewed down his neck. "Do not let this monster survive! Usuthu, black demon, I charge you to seal my revenge."

His last words were lost in a gargling of blood. His body broke in two with a crunch.

The dragon consumed Thormod and considered the ship again. Usuthu leaned back. With a fierce cry he rocked forward and, still sitting on the heaving deck, hurled the lance with a sweeping overhand toss. His huge wrist flicked gracefully as he released the blade.

The dragon ducked to one side but the spear, driven by a chance gust, seemed to follow it down. The blade took the beast squarely in its eye. Hot, steaming yellow blood gushed forth and drenched the ship. It stank of bile and blood, and worse. Berserk with pain and rage, the dragon snatched at the ship with its jaws. It caught the mast and sail and destroyed them with one bite. The ship, free of the surge of the wind, stopped dead in the water and turned broadside to an onrushing swell.

The dragon, mortally wounded but far from done, dragged its huge head across the deck, trailing what remained of the mast and sail. Kirstin, the youngest and most foolish man aboard, flung himself onto the dragon's back. Clutching the serpent's neck with his knees, he raised his broadsword before him, gripping it with two hands. As the beast reared he plunged the gleaming blade in to the hilt. Kirstin vanished in a fountain spray of yellow blood.

The monster stood straight up in the water and fell over backward, carrying Kirstin with it. There was a great splash. Then only the sound of the wind.

"To the oars!" screamed Janor. "We've turned to!"

Every hand, save Usuthu, leaped for an empty chest and slid the nearest oar into the sea.

"Pull to the wind." cried Mälar.

The men dropped their shoulders and grunted as one. A wave broke over the ship, lifting it high upon one side. The *Freyja* adjusted like a bird in flight, and slid down the back side of the crest that had almost engulfed her. Janor swung the tiller one way as the wave passed beneath them. When the ship was clear he swung the rudder back the other way just as the crew pulled in one long stroke. Magically the bow came around, right into the wind.

Halberd's wounded arm prevented him from rowing. Clutching the lifeline, he made his way to the stern.

"Mälar, you must row. I'll help Janor with my one good arm."

Mälar, the old war-horse, took his seat on a chest without grumbling. He had sailed for adventure. His adventure was to be, like many, endless hard work in the name of survival. The younger crew members were not so resilient. They complained loudly as the hours of rowing passed. Usuthu sat in the prow, studying the waves, trying to learn the way of the sea. Hour after hour he stared into the gray crests.

The wind shifted to their stern and the sea before them flattened. They seemed to have reached the Western Current. Halberd called half the crew off the oars. Six exhausted men fell into their furs and were soon asleep. Mälar ordered Janor to rest and took the helm himself. His skinny old frame masked great endurance. Halberd felt a rush of admiration and gratitude for the shipwright. Warriors like Mälar had earned the Northmen the respect of the Known World.

Usuthu called Halberd to the bow.

"I cannot fathom the magic of the sea," he said wearily. "I am of no use aboard this vessel. My body must stay here but my spirit cannot. Bind me once again."

Halberd and Labrans tied the giant Mongol to the jagged stump of the mast. Usuthu sat upon a sleeping fur with his legs lolling free. His chest was tied tightly to the stump. He closed his eyes and entered a deep trance.

The crew rowed in shifts and slept as they could. Three days and nights dragged by. In the dead of the third night, when even the waking oarsmen nodded over their shafts, a tiny spout of flame appeared on the horizon.

"Wake, wake!" cried Janor the Insane. "The land melts and the mountains explode. Wake!"

The crew rolled from their skins and made for the prow. As the current bore them westward the Isle of Fire grew larger and larger just off their northwest bow. The Isle of Fire was a permanently melting and reforming land of great volcanoes. The burning mountains hurled stones as large as villages into the sky. Earth, as red as flame and liquid as water, ran down their sides and bubbled into the sea, throwing plumes of steam hundreds of feet into the air. As the *Freyja* neared the island the air grew warmer, and the Western Current swifter.

Halberd urged Janor to steer as near to the burning rock as he could. When they were no more than a league away Halberd cast off his furs and, clinging to a lifeline, leaped into the sea. His younger crew members gasped, but Mälar and Janor only smiled.

"Tie yourselves to the ship and come on," Halberd told them. "The sea is as warm as a bath."

And so the edge of the Sea of Blackness passed in laughter and splashing, as the men of the

Freyja forgot their perilous journey. They drew refreshment from the warm bath and clambered back on board reluctantly, cursing as they dressed again in their soaking furs.

The crew gathered around Halberd near the stern so that all might hear. Relax, they chewed their rations and listened with care.

"Once past the Isle of Fire," Halberd began, "we have moved beyond the boundaries of the Known World. As the Western Current grows stronger we will pass into the Great Open Ocean. Once there it is a matter of days to Vinland. None but the Great-Great-Grandfathers and Valdane have ever come beyond this point.

"We will row in shifts. The current is potent and will bear us west as we need. I will stand the helm, but my first duty is to enter the Dreaming World. I must find our course and determine if any of my brother's force remains alive."

"What about the demon?" asked Gardar, the largest man in Halberd's village before Usuthu's arrival.

"What demon?" Halberd replied, his voice as icy as the sea.

"The black demon who sleeps by the mast! What evil does he conjure? Every time we subdue him with rope a new serpent appears. We should kill him as he sleeps."

Halberd stood wearily. He had not slept fully in three nights. His arm pained him. With his good arm he gingerly pulled his dagger from its sheath. Holding it lightly, turning it over and over with his fingertips, he looked up at Gardar.

"Before you kill him in his sleep, brave one,

kill me as I stand half awake." Halberd felt the bloodlust rise in him as never before. He was a warrior as well as a holy man.

"I bear you no malice, shaman," said Gardar, drawing his own long knife carefully. "But I fear you neither. If I kill you I wonder if we can find our way back home against this current, but I will not back away from your challenge."

The crew formed a ragged circle. Most looked undecided. All held their own weapons uneasily, uncertain of the next step to take. Gardar slid toward Halberd, one foot forward, his knife held close to his hip. Halberd stood calmly, his weight balanced on both feet. The dank sea breeze blew softly over the men.

The circle of crewmen parted briefly. There was a flurry of motion which Halberd could not see. Gardar pitched forward onto his face. He hit the decking with a thud and bounced. He lay still.

Smiling behind the prostrate form of Gardar was Mälar. He brandished the oar with which he had clouted Gardar.

"Back to your posts, brave Northmen," he said. "Demon or no, the black giant is our crewmate and we all must protect our fellow warriors, like it or not."

Staring each man in the eye as he left the circle, Mälar made sure they understood: to challenge Halberd was to challenge Mälar.

"Young shaman, you are spent. Sleep near the tiller. We will watch over you," Mälar smiled.

Halberd took his advice. Huddled into his furs at Janor's feet, he closed his eyes.

Halberd sees Vinland. The low gray shore is unmarked and endless. Halberd peers deeper into the gray light, searching for a landmark. As he does a face appears. Beckoning and smiling, the face grows clearer. It is the lovely woman from his vision dream. She has long black hair framing a dusky face with almond-shaped eyes which glow as black as coals. Her skin is soft brown, her teeth dazzlingly white and even. The sight of her fills Halberd with love. She seems so familiar, so kind, so trustworthy. Again he reaches to touch her. This time he is able to rest his fingers on her soft, warm skin for an instant. His heart aches at the touch of her face. He calls to her. She smiles.

Halberd looked up from his furs. The night sky was clear. The ship raced forward, borne as if by full sail. The air was frigid, colder than during the ice storm. The woman's smile gave Halberd a deep sense of peace and contentment that warmed him like a fire. He did not need to see the Jewel to know this dream was true.

"Where are we?" Halberd spoke to the massive feet of Janor, which were right beside Halberd's head.

Janor jumped as if touched with a firebrand. "Oh ho, my prophet! You awaken."

"How long have I slept?"

"Only three days, three days, no more." Janor laughed and stamped his feet.

"As to where we are," said Mälar, who stood behind Janor, "I cannot say. All stars that we steer by are far behind us. I am charting the new ones, and I know we still sail west. And north, I think. The cold is increasing."

Halberd went forward. The deck was a single sheet of ice. The lines were coated with it. Sleeping Northmen were shrouded under it. Usuthu, still as death, was covered with a thick sheet of the frozen sea. No part of him was visible.

Halberd put a hand against the clear shell. Closing his eyes, he listened hard for a heartbeat. Usuthu's heart sounded like a drum. The drumming sound grew louder and louder in Halberd's ear. The drumbeats became hoofs striking the ground at high speed. The ship vanished and Halberd found himself on the Great Steppes, racing over the endless prairie on a fast horse. On the ridge lay a vast camp of tents, yurts, warriors and women. Fires burned brightly, and even at twilight, the summer sun was strong.

Halberd withdrew his hand. The summer camp disappeared. Halberd understood. Usuthu had left his body on the ship and sent his spirit back to the camp of his people. He was using the warmth of the summer camp to stay alive.

The crew were sullen. Days at sea had sapped their will. This was no quick raid, with plunder, women, and the glory of battle. Exploration was dull and dangerous. No one but Halberd knew if the Vinland camp existed, or even if the vast island itself lay before them. They might miss it and sail beyond the Great Open Ocean. And what lay there no one could guess. The wind dropped and the entire crew were called to oars. Glad for something to do to ward off the cold, they pulled mightily.

The next morning, a cold day under dark clouds, Labrans, in the prow, spied land. The crew pulled feverishly, seaching for some clue. In half a day they lay just offshore.

The land was icy gray, covered with glaciers and set behind forbidding cliffs of sheer green ice. The crew were downcast. There were no trees, no beach, no birds and no sound. The *Freyja* moved as near to the shore as possible and sailed south, following the contours of the land.

Halberd dreamed once more. The face has returned. The beautiful young woman fills the sky. She beams at Halberd with love and speaks for the first time, but Halberd cannot understand her words.

"Can you hear me?" he calls, and his voice echoes to the edge of the universe.

She nods, smiling broadly.

"Do you know my name?"

Again, she smiles.

"And my quest."

The beautiful young woman nodded again, gravely.

"Do you know the witch Grettir?"

She nods again, the look of a frightened deer in her wide, black eyes.

"Should I fear her?"

A single short nod.

"Will you guide us to our camp?"

The young woman, her face beaming with love, extends her hand and points to the horizon. Her other hand reaches for Halberd. He longs to clasp her hand, but their fingertips remain inches apart. Halberd strains, but he cannot close the gap. She smiles tenderly.

"Wait!"

But again, she was gone.

Halberd awoke and surveyed his crew. They gazed back at him without a word. They needed fresh food, a dry place to sleep, the earth under their feet again. For two days they had drifted along this horrible coastline, waiting for some sign. If he was their leader, it was up to him to lead.

Halberd knelt over the ice-covered form of Usuthu.

"Awake, my brother," Halberd said softly. "I need you."

After a moment, cracks appeared in the thick ice that sheathed the Mongol. A crack ran from his head to his waist. Another began at his toes and shot crazily up his legs. A larger fissure opened in the dirty gray ice on his chest. Usuthu raised his ice-covered head. The ice surrounding him exploded outward, blasting shards over Halberd, cutting his face. Pieces of jagged ice, sharp as glass, sailed past the startled crew. They leaped from their chests, reaching for swords, unsure as to the exact nature of this fearsome magic.

Halberd wiped the last bits of ice from Usuthu's face.

"Water," the giant croaked.

Janor, unafraid, came forward with a drinking skin. He held it to Usuthu's mouth as the Mongol drank greedily.

"Free me," he whispered, when his thirst was quenched.

Janor took a small bronze razor from his tunic and slashed the frozen ropes in an instant. The crew looked on, unable to move. Mälar held the tiller, unconcerned.

"Help me stand."

Halberd and Janor together, pulling with all their strength, could not raise Usuthu on his weak legs.

"Help us, you cowards," Halberd called, his voice stinging like a lash.

Gardar sprang from his chest. Laying aside his sword, he grabbed Usuthu by one massive wrist and yanked him to his feet single-handed. As the Mongol toppled forward, Gardar put his own strong hands on the giant's chest and propped him up.

Halberd looked into Gardar's eyes. "You are no coward, my friend. I acted in haste by challenging you. I extend my arm in fealty and ask your forgiveness."

"There is nothing to forgive," Gardar said quietly, so that the crew would not hear their exchange. "We are Northmen and do not remember petty squabbles when action is required."

Leaning against Usuthu to hold him up, Gardar extended his arm to Halberd. Halberd clasped his wrist in friendship.

"I can stand," Usuthu whispered. "Give me my bow."

Halberd held it out to him.

"And an arrow."

Usuthu rested the arrow on the deck and bent to string his bow. It required all his strength. Halberd watched, speechless. He did not know what fueled Usuthu's terrible resolve. Usuthu bent the bow back with agonizing slowness. His hands shook. Once, twice, he tried to slip the string into the notch.

Gazing to the heavens, muttering a short prayer under his breath, he tried a third time. The bowstring slid home. The watching crew released their held breath as one man. Usuthu drew himself to his full majestic height. He nocked the arrow and straightened his bow arm.

Standing tall, he studied the featureless coastline for a long time. The crew did not move or speak.

Usuthu turned to Mälar, who held the helm.

"Mark you well," Usuthu said.

He turned and fired his arrow toward the coast. It soared far into the low, gray sky and came down behind a towering cliff of ice.

"Follow it," the Mongol said. "There lies our camp."

He collapsed on the deck, spent.

Mälar adjusted the course. The crew bent to their oars.

BOOK TWO

Vinland

Skrælings

Gray water lapped at gray ice. The *Freyja* moved within an oar's length of the endless ice cliff and slowly slid along it. Mälar stood in the prow, peering under his flattened hand at the featureless ice wall, searching for landmarks. Usuthu sat by the shattered mast, eating dried fish, regaining his strength. Halberd waited by the tiller with Janor, one hand resting on the head of his battleax.

The clouds moved lower and began to gather. A thick but gentle snow fell. The light was flat and gray. Distance became impossible to gauge. Time and again oars rasped against the cliff wall as Janor let the *Freyja* drift too close. Oars snapped in two when a sudden gust shoved the ship hard upon the gray-green ice.

Mälar straightened and thrust his right arm out from his body, pointing at the cliff.

"Now!" he screamed.

Janor swung the rudder instantly. The ship pivoted in less than half its length and the prow came around sharply to precisely the place Mälar had pointed. The snow blew thicker now, and neither Janor nor Halberd could see where they were going.

"Up oars," cried Halberd. The crew raised their oars out of the water. For the first time since Usuthu had fired his arrow, they raised their heads and peered through the snow.

The prow scraped the icy cliff, bumped it again, rebounded and hit once more. The *Freyja* slid back from the wall.

Mälar, in the prow, spoke in a whisper: "Pull gently now, gently."

The oarsmen laid their blades in the water. As one they drew a deep breath.

"Stroke," whispered Mälar.

The oars moved like leaves across a pond. Where they touched, tiny, soft whirlpools spun in the flat gray sea. The oars drew one stroke and hung, poised, over the sea.

"And again," called Mälar, his voice barely audible.

Matching the strength of their pull to the volume of the call, the crew pulled softly.

Halberd knelt by Usuthu and looked up through thick flakes toward the wall. The snow blinded him. He took another step forward.

"Once more," came the hoarse whisper. Like a timid horse, the *Freyja* took one tiny step.

The snow ceased. The wind stopped. The sea made no sound. Nor did any member of the crew. The men held their oars straight up. Every jaw hung open.

The *Freyja* rested in the mouth of a tiny cut in the cliff. The cut was barely wider than the ship. Walls of ice, three times as tall as the ship was long, towered overhead. Far, far above them, a tiny patch of gray sky showed at the top of the cliff walls. Driven deep into the wall at the opening of the cut, surrounded by spiral cracks, was Usuthu's arrow.

The crew stared, awe-struck. No fjord in the Northland had walls so high, sheer, or narrow.

"This is a giant ice cave, lacking only a roof." Halberd was surprised he had spoken aloud.

"No," said Mälar. "These walls are floes of ice, squeezed together by the cold and the sea."

"I fear not." Labrans spoke from the bow, his tone heavy with dread. "This must be the entrance to a fortress. Or a trap. Others have come before us. Behold."

Two ship lengths ahead the cut took a sharp bend. No one could see what lay beyond it. The crew looked from man to man, reading the determination or fear to be found in the face of their fellows.

"Ship oars," Mälar barked.

The oars were slid aboard and laid on the deck. The locks had been destroyed by the serpent.

"Prepare to pole."

The crew raised their spears. The walls of the cut were near enough to touch. Each man stood and laid a spearpoint into the ice. They waited for the command.

"What is this place, Usuthu?" Halberd whispered, fearful that the crew might hear some horrible reply.

"The place of your brother's ghost."

"Then let it be a trap," Halberd said. His words echoed off the ice walls. "We go forward."

Near the prow, Labrans leaned against his spear, pressing the steel point into the ice wall. The ice was so thick and brittle the spear did not penetrate. Labrans raised the spear and jammed it into the cliff. The sharpened point bent and then snapped clean away. Labrans looked at his fractured spearpoint carefully. He had driven that very blade through the iron armor of a Lyndisfarne knight. On horseback, no less! The blade had punctured the knight's armor, gone through him as he screamed, out his back and armor again without scratching the blade. The smiths who lived near the Guardian Rock which stood at the entrance to the Inland Sea had made that blade. They were the finest smiths in the Known World.

Yet the ice had broken it. Usuthu had driven an arrow into this ice! The crew examined their own blades and looked back at Usuthu. He sat on the deck, eating, unaware of their stares. The *Freyja* waited in the mouth of the cut, umoving. Labrans walked past Halberd and Usuthu to the stern. Leaning over the gunwale, he reached up and tried to draw Usuthu's arrow from the ice. It did not move. Grabbing the shaft with both hands, Labrans swung out of the boat. Hanging from the arrow, dangling over the flat gray water, Labrans raised and lowered himself rapidly.

"Labrans, my brother," Halberd called softly, "what mischief are you making for Usuthu? Do not call attention to his magic."

Labrans hauled himself up the arrow to the level of his chin one more time. Rocking back and forth, he swung off the arrow and landed on the deck in a catlike crouch. Labrans had always been deft.

"Little brother, do not order me about," he hissed. "I am your elder and will do as I please."

Halberd stepped backward. Customarily, Labrans spoke very little. It was his nature. He and Valdane had never been close, but as children they also had seldom argued. Labrans was right in one sense; the younger brother had no right to order the elder. But the war-chief of an expedition must have obedience from his crew. Halberd was baffled by his brother's hostility.

"Take my spear, brother," Halberd said. "I am sorry for my harsh tone."

The crew, clustered in the prow, watched the exchange carefully. With land so near, they felt less dependent on Halberd, Mälar, and Janor the Insane. If their leader was about to be challenged by one with a natural right of control, such as an older brother, the crew was prepared to follow.

Labrans studied his younger brother. Stooping, he picked up his broken spear. Saying nothing, he turned and strode to the prow.

Halberd felt an odd sense of danger. He saw Usuthu looking over his shoulder. Halberd glanced up and saw nothing. He reached above his head and yanked his broadword out of its scabbard.

Nestled in its web of silver, the Jewel of Krywyn-Coyne glowed softly in the gray light.

Halberd could make no sense of it. Usuthu observed the Jewel with a somber face.

"Perhaps the Dream World is invading this world," Halberd said, half to himself and half to Usuthu. They stared at the Jewel as its glow slowly faded.

Halberd knelt next to Usuthu so none could hear.

"Perhaps Grettir is watching us from the Dream World. Perhaps she is near still. She may never have fled to the Unknown World."

"Perhaps Grettir attempts to inhabit your brother," Usuthu said. "He is not a playful man, yet he frolics with danger so near. Then he challenges you before your crew."

"We must watch for new enemies in this land," Halberd said.

"Go, go, go," cried Janor. "We cannot linger at the mouth of this cliff. We must go into the gray dark, though with all my soul I would not."

"Aye," cried Mälar. "Fear grows with lack of motion. Any true sailor hates a calm. It's time to pole. Brace yourselves."

The crew leaned their spear blades into the ice on either side of the ship.

"Pole!" Mälar's voice blew along the ice cliffs, surrounded the ship with a hundred Mälars, then faded away. After an apprehensive look around, the crew bent their shoulders to their spears and pushed off.

The *Freyja* moved swiftly down the narrow cut.

Mälar raised his hand once more. The crew put their speartips to the wall, waiting.

"Hold!" whispered Halberd. Everyone turned from the bow to stare.

"Put down your spears," Halberd whispered. "We do not know this place and we will not go in like lambs. Every man make for his arms and prepare himself for war."

The crew left their spears by the prow and returned to their rowing stations. The *Freyja* rocked quietly in the cut. The gray walls loomed over the ship, seeming to draw even closer. Every sound the ship made echoed crazily up the walls and rebounded down upon the heads of the crew. They moved with exaggerated care and, as a result, made even more noise. Every man produced his own leather-and-steel armor, his shield and his weapon of choice. Some wore huge broadswords, some axes, some vicious maces with ten-pound, spike-studded iron heads, some simple war-clubs taken from the Heathmen in earlier raids. All were set with jewels or precious metal, some were carved with animals and others with names or faces of loved ones.

Every man had a bow, of course, and these were rested on the gunwales near the prow. Each crew member slid his shield on his arm. They stood taller now, and worried less about the constant echo.

A push from the crew and the *Freyja* reached the right-angle turn in the cut. The prow went in first and then the crew, shoving with their hands upon the ice walls, guided the ship around the bend. They were now fully committed. To back up through this turn would be almost impossible. To do so under attack, suicidal. They must go forward.

As they pushed along the ice, the top of the cliff walls drew nearer. The walls were smaller in height. Soon they were no more than one ship length above. The snow now blew in on the *Freyja* once more.

The sky was more visible, but no end to the ice maze was in sight. Many twists and turns were negotiated. The cut never widened or narrowed. Great white bears patrolled the tops of the cliffs, the only visible signs of life. They stood on their hind legs and roared at the Northmen, who only glanced up and kept up their pace. They had seen white bears before.

Another right angle was negotiated. The cliff walls were even lower now, no more than four or five man-heights above the ship. Once through the bend the *Freyja* stopped once more.

Ahead was the end of the cut. The walls simply stopped and the water pushed quietly against a gentle slope of dirty frozen snow. Rocking in the quiet water was the burned-out hulk of a ship, unmistakably a dragonhead Northman ocean vessel. The ship had been burned down to the waterline. Only the blackened spars of the keel and the ribs of the hull remained. The charcoaled ruin was tethered to a two-handed Northman harpoon driven deep into the frozen snow.

"We have found Valdane's ship," Mälar announced.

"Prepare to beach," Halberd called softly. The sight of the burned ship had provoked new depths of fear in the crew. They moved reluctantly, staring at the charred shell, looking for some sign of its fate.

"Thorsten, climb ashore and pull us in. You have the warmest feet," Mälar ordered.

Thorsten, a young warrior famous for always being the first off any boat in any attack in any weather, sprang over the prow and landed in the knee-deep frigid water with a great splash. The crew, huddled in the prow around their spears, threw him down a line and he trudged the last few steps through the water and onto the snow slope. With one mighty yank he drew the prow of the *Freyja* onto the snow. The front few feet of the ship slid onto land.

A moist crunching sound turned everyone toward the stern.

Janor stood by his tiller. Protruding from his chest was six inches of shaft and the barbed ivory point of a massive whaling harpoon. Flecks of skin and blood hung from the barbed point. The wooden shaft stuck out behind him and fastened to it a long line hung in loose loops in the air, disappearing up and behind the cliff wall.

Janor took the shaft with both hands and sank to his knees. He tugged gently at the barbed point, trying to dislodge it. He opened his mouth to cry out, and a large bright-red bubble formed on his lips. It burst as he gasped horribly, and blood exploded down his chest. Behind him, the line tightened.

With great effort Janor turned his head to look at the line. The dangling loops were vanishing slowly as someone pulled on the line from behind the safety of the clifftop.

"Do not let the line tighten, my brothers!"

Janor gurgled. A new gout of blood splashed down his front as he tried to speak. "They seek to pull me straight to Niflheim. Let the line stay slack! I must have slack to live! I must have slack!"

He vomited another burst of blood as he screamed.

The line tightened straight as an arrow. Janor was snatched backward off the deck before any man could move. He sailed through the air as if weightless.

"Slack," he said, quietly, beyond any hope or any insanity, now.

The force with which he was yanked drew him crashing into the wall. The haft of the harpoon struck the wall first, driving three more feet of ivory shaft and wooden handle through his chest. Janor raised his head to scream a final time, but was porcupined with arrows before he could make a sound.

His unseen attackers whisked him up and over the clifftop with a final gruesome bump against the lip of the cliff. Janor vanished.

Halberd looked to Mälar, who looked to Usuthu, who looked to Bjarni, who looked over the prow to Thorsten. Almost every member of the crew held an empty bow in his hands. All had fired as Janor hung, arms and legs splayed wide, against the cliff wall. A great bloody smear testified to his moment of death.

All knew that a warrior, captured and tortured, and possibly eaten alive, could never be granted entry to Aasgard. A Northman thus dispatched would be cast to Niflheim, there to answer to the fearsome god of the underworld, Hel and his demon servant, Nidhogg.

Likewise, all knew that a wounded warrior, killed out of mercy by his brothers in arms, died with honor intact and soul bound for the maidens, wine, and constant glorious battle that was Aasgard.

Death in battle was nothing new to the Northman. But Janor seemed sainted by his insanity. He had ridden at the fore of every battle, collected great amounts of booty, and slain many enemies. Halberd had known Janor since his youth. Janor had taught him much in the way of war. Usuthu, too, seemed shocked. Janor was a Northman that Usuthu had elected to understand. He never spoke to Janor, but would huddle by his fire and listen avidly, hour after hour.

The crew stood disconsolate and disorganized. The *Freyja* was partway upon the snowy beach, yet no man moved to bring her ashore. Bows hung from arms drooping to the deck, and every head studied either the bloody smear on the wall or the empty bows in their hands.

Halberd roused himself. He dropped his bow to the deck and took his hair in his hands. But for the awful burden of leading the crew, he would have wept. He drew a deep breath. A loud thump from the deck next to him caused him to jump aside.

Another missile crashed into the deck with a thump and then a bouncing sound. Halberd wearily looked upward. Apparently an arctic hailstorm had moved in. They would have to hide under their shields until it passed. Then he saw Usuthu take a stone the size of a sheep's paunch in the shield Usuthu wore upon his chest. It should have knocked him down but it did not. It simply bent his shield down in a great curve. Any other man would have been killed.

Another stone crashed into the deck, and then another.

"We are attacked by war-slings!" Mälar cried. "To the rollers and move up the beach."

Every man leaped for his oar, oblivious to the hail of stones. Each grabbed an oar and sprang over the prow. Laying the oars in a line upon the snow, perpendicular to the *Freyja*, they dragged the graceful craft right up the snow slope, using the oars as rollers. Usuthu, Halberd, and Mälar pulled on the *Freyja*'s lead line, while every crewman stood by his oar. As soon as the *Freyja* passed over it, he would grab his oar and run to the front of the ship. There he would fling the oar under it once again and wait for the ship to slid over its smooth and rounded shaft.

All stood on the side of the *Freyja* away from the sling attack, and so none were hurt. All could hear the damage their craft absorbed protecting them. None could see their attackers. They stayed well hidden behind the wall of the ice cliff.

After several breathless ship lengths had been pulled, Halberd sank to his knees to draw a gasping breath. Mälar knelt beside him. The attack had ceased.

"Look here," said Halberd. "The cliffs run out at the end of the cut. We are on the edge of a great ice plain."

"And the beach beyond," Mälar replied, "a league to the south, seems to be at the edge of a lagoon formed by the ice cliffs. Here they are not hard upon the shore, but protect it like a fortress wall. Yet this beach, from this distance, appears black. Why would this be?"

"Because," Usuthu answered, peering under a flattened hand from his great height, "The beach is made of black stones, not ice, nor sand, nor snow."

"What did he say?" Mälar asked Halberd.

"He said that there, upon that beach, lies the body of my brother."

Labrans, resting among the crew, pointed up the snowy plain on which they now stood. At the crest of a long gentle rise, not more than twenty ship lengths away, stood, unmistakably, a Northman stone greathouse.

"There is Valdane's fortress." Labrans said. "There we must find his crew."

"Back to harness," called Mälar.

He, Halberd, and Usuthu picked up the rope as the crew readied to move their oars.

"Hold!" screamed Bjarni from the rear of the *Freyja.* "Skrælings!"

Boiling up from behind the cliff walls and spilling down onto the short snowy plain which separated the *Freyja* from the end of the cut were dozens upon dozens of short squat men, all armed with ivory spears, all clad head to foot in baggy furs, all with broad faces and slitted eyes. All were screaming in an incomprehensible and terrifying tongue. They were bent on murder.

Northmen did not need orders to fight for their lives, nor to deal with any enemy. They did not fight in formation unless all took the same idea in their heads at the same moment. Here, that occurred.

With Usuthu, the largest, at the rear, the crew formed two ranks in order of height. The front rank knelt and the rear rank stood. All nocked arrows and waited for the screaming horde to come within range. Gardar, the largest and strongest after Usuthu, Mälar, not a particularly good shot, and Halberd, whose bow was still aboard the *Freyja*, knelt before the front rank. Each held a lance toward the onrushing Skrælings. They would be the first to engage the demons hand to hand.

Usuthu fired before the first Skræling had cleared the end of the cliff wall. His arrow struck the leader in the chest and hurled him backward so strongly that he knocked over three of his charging fellows. Before those four had even struck the ground Usuthu had launched three more arrows.

The first of those took a Skræling just under his chin. The arrow went through and killed the barbarian racing behind him, thrusting into his chest and pinning him to the frozen snow. He thrashed about in his baggy furs, his blood soaking the snow around him.

The next three arrows whacked their targets flat into the snow. The brutal thumps of the arrows' stone heads passing through thick fur rose over the screams of the Skrælings.

The front rank of screaming demons was decimated by Usuthu's arrows, yet the party did not stop or even look back to consider their dead.

"They behave oddly," Mälar shouted to Halberd over the din. "Savages cannot endure death on this scale. Tribes are small and every warrior lost a tragedy."

"Yes, either their numbers are vast or they are unlike any savages we have ever fought." Halberd shouted back. "Also, these barbarians do not fight for honor, but to annihilate us."

The Northmen were puzzled. Usually demons and savages did not seek to wipe out an enemy. They did not care for tactics. Customarily they would attack in small numbers, commit some feat of suicidal daring, and melt away. Savages seldom engaged a foe of any size face to face. Yet this attack force seemed uninterested in their own well-being or in victory. They apparently desired only the destruction of the Northmen.

"I believe they wish us eliminated no matter what the cost," Halberd shouted to Mälar.

"Why would this be so?"

"They fear us. I believe they think we are the demons."

"Why should they fear us? Mälar answered. "They do not know us. They could not know of us before our landing."

"How else could they assemble a force of this size or lances in this number?" Halberd spoke into Mälar's ear. "I fear that somehow Grettir told them to expect us."

"If that is so, her power is greater than that of any mortal I have ever known."

* * *

The gap between the two small armies narrowed. The Skrælings carried no bows, only their ivory lances. They ran forward across the dirty gray snow, still screaming.

Just outside of bow range, still well beyond the toss of a lance, the Skrælings stopped. Each savage produced a short, hollowed-out length of wood from his furs. The butt of their lances fit into these wood shafts. They raised the shafts into throwing position and let fly. The holders remained in their hands yet granted tremendous power to their throws. The light spears sailed into the sky and carried farther than any Northman had ever seen a spear thrown. The barbed spears whistled down upon the Northmen. They dropped their bows and raised their shields to the sky. The light shafts bounced off the leather-and-iron shields, causing injury to no one.

Though the Northmen were held motionless as the shafts rained down upon them, the Skrælings did not advance. Again, they seemed afraid of coming too near to the Northmen.

"Up and charge them," cried Gardar. "We must fill them with arrows before they strike again."

The Northmen rose into one rank and rushed toward the Skrælings, who stood their ground and calmly fitted more spears into their odd holders. After twenty paces or so, the Northmen all drew bows and let fly without pausing to kneel. A solid mass of arrows filled the air.

The effect was devastating. Almost every arrow found a target. Where two men had chosen the same demon when aiming their target was pinned to the frozen ground, twin shafts rising from his blood-spattered fur. Well over sixty Skrælings had charged moments before and now fewer than twenty-five remained. Their leader waved his arms and the survivors let fly with another volley of ivory-tipped spears.

But the instant these had left their arms the Northmen had charged again, moving forward under the trajectory of the whistling missiles. As the spears struck the ground behind them the Northmen loosed another volley of arrows at the rank of Skrælings. Another ten or twelve went down.

Far behind the Vikings, at their original position, Usuthu still stood, calmly choosing his arrows and letting fly. With every shot, another Skræling was nailed through to the snow. With the front rank so decimated, Usuthu had time to aim behing them, picking off the walking wounded and the few who were starting to flee.

As this volley struck home, Mälar, Halberd, and Gardar drew their axes and charged the Skrælings, each sounding his own battle-cry. At this the Skrælings broke and ran for the shelter of the ice cliff. The Northmen gave their fleeing backs another volley. Half were cut down. Usuthu, now far behind, thoughtfullly lowered his bow.

"Cease, cease!" shouted Halberd, waving his arms. "Let one or two live, to spread the word of our power and victory."

The crew lowered their bows and stared at Halberd dumbly. These were the first spoken words or rational thoughts since the battle had been joined. Their blood raced. The desire to see every Skræling dead was strong. Their chests heaved and their arms ached. They examined one another carefully for wounds and saw only scratches. They had won a great victory.

"Move among them with care," called Mälar. "Take your arrows back from the dead, dispatch the mortally wounded, and send those still alive on their way. Gather even the ivory lances. We require every weapon. On this barren plain lies little wood for shipbuilding and even less for arrows."

"Halberd," called Usuthu from his place on the gentle hill. "Collect every idol these barbarians carry and make them fuel for a fire. This must be done swiftly. Make sure the survivors can see the blaze and that which is fed to it."

With those words he started forward to pull his arrows from the dead demons.

"What did he say this time" asked Labrans sullenly.

"He said," replied Mälar, "that we should demonstrate to the Skrælings the superiority of our gods as well as our arms. Search the dead and living for any idols and make a fire of them here on the Plain of Death. They shall see that no demon may challenge us."

Half the crew ignored this exchange, intent as they were on wrenching their arrows from the bodies of the Skrælings. Many shafts had gone right through the demons and required considerable labor to pull free. The Northmen propped one fur-booted foot on the carcasses of their fallen foes and heaved with all their strength. The arrows came free to a chorus of gruesome creaking and snapping as bones and ligaments broke along the backward path of the retrieved arrows.

Those not too far gone with the bloody work stared back at Mälar in amazement. Even Halberd was stunned.

"You understand this giant?" asked Gardar.

"Yes, and perfectly," came the confident reply.

"How, Mälar?" asked Labrans. "Are you now possessed by him?"

Halberd stood by without interfering. He did not know how Mälar could have made such a discovery. Even Janor never understood the language of the Steppes.

"I do not know. Some years before I sailed many journeys to the Land of Sand on the Inland Sea. There I met representatives of Usuthu's people and spent much time at their fire, discussing their gods and mine. At the time we used the language of the black-skinned slave traders, which all civilized men know. But I listened when they spoke among themselves and have been carefully remembering all of their words. Now I feel that a veil is lifting between my ears and Usuthu. I cannot speak his language, but I understand much of what he says."

"You are possessed of him," spat Thorsten. "I fear you as I do him and I will trust you as little."

"Thorsten," answered Mälar easily, "you are a child and as such I cannot in good conscience snatch your liver from your bowels and feed it into your large and flapping mouth. However, tomorrow you will be one day older than today. I declare, then, that tomorrow you shall have attained your manhood. If you wish to repeat yourself when the sun rises next, do so on those terms."

"Hold, brothers," said Labrans. "As Mälar has said before, we are crewmates and must make our way in this hostle land for months to come. We must not quarrel. Gardar has made his peace with the black demon, and you, Thorsten, shall do the same. Now."

"But just moments before you questioned this strange event as well," Thorsten sputtered to Labrans.

An icy glance from Labrans' hooded eyes silenced the young warrior.

"I will say no more on this matter at any time," Thorsten said, turning away to fetch his arrows. He drew his club from his belt and looked eagerly among the sprawling, fur-clad bodies, hoping for a wounded prisoner. His rage at Labrans and Mälar would find expression in the flesh of the Skrælings.

"Why this change of heart, Labrans?" asked Halberd. "I know you do not trust Usuthu."

"My words are forged on the anvil not of trust, but of staying alive in the coming months. Your demon is stronger than any three of us. I need him to live. I will not have him harmed." Labrans strode away.

Usuthu had reached Halberd and Mälar. They watched Labrans stroll casually across the field of carnage. Halberd pulled his broadsword from its scabbard and examined the Jewel of Kyrwyn-Coyne. Again, it glowed.

"Labrans' actions are as puzzling as the glow of

this Jewel," said Halberd. "He changes his course with every breath. I fear he is being controlled from the Dream World and will no longer be my brother in any form. Soon I must sleep and learn more."

"Another aspect of this battle which none have raised," said Mälar, "is the absence of any aid or message from the greathouse. Either the surviving crew is away on a hunt, which seems unlikely in this weather, or . . ."

"Or they are all dead," interrupted Halberd. "I never believed we would find a single one of them alive. In my dream I saw that Valdane alone had survived a gruesome battle. That battle wiped out his men."

"What will occur," asked Usuthu, "When this crew learns the fate of that one?"

"They will fear us even more and yet believe that they must rely heavily on our judgment to stay alive," said Mälar grimly. "Such a combination will breed great hatred. We cannot stay on this icy rock until spring. We must leave as soon as possible."

"And so," said Halberd, "we shall."

They joined the men and soon had a collection of arrows and ivory lances. Next to these was a remarkable assortment of idols and figures. As they moved from body to body, rolling each dead barbarian onto his back, helping some wounded to their feet and sending them toward the ice cliff, finishing others with a swift dagger thrust or mace swing, they searched in the furs for figures of the Skræling gods. Some wounded protested in a thick, guttural tongue. They did not want to be parted from their idols. One or two drew knives and tried to slash the arms of their captors to retrieve their idols. These quickly joined their rapidly stiffening brothers.

Halberd moved through the field of corpses. One had rested lightly on the handle of his dagger. His men were thorough. There was no reason to believe that any in this snowy plain remained alive. Halberd examined the Skrælings with great care.

They were short and squat, but powerful. Their hair was long and black and their faces broad and unpleasant to look upon. Their cheekbones were wide and their eyes slitted. They appeared to be distant relatives of Usuthu. Despite their ugliness, their wrinkled faces bore the same savage, unshakable dignity.

Loose fur tunics, pulled over the head, covered their upper bodies, and baggy fur trousers protected their legs. Thick fur boots covered their feet and lower legs up to the knee. These seemed better designed for the cold and wet than the fur wrappings the Northmen wore. Halberd finished his inspection and went back to the growing pile of idols.

A large crowd of Skrælings had gathered on the ice cliff to watch. Among the huge force of warriors were women and children. The Northmen were concerned about this growing army, but moved to their tasks without showing fear. They would show the Skrælings their bravery and willingness to fight.

Also it was twilight. Few savage tribes were willing to fight after dark. Indeed, even the Northmen preferred a warm fire once the sun had set.

"Halberd," said Mälar, "look here. The Skrælings had good reason to fear us and even to expect our arrival. They are well acquainted with Grettir."

Mälar passed a small ivory carved figure to Halberd. It was unmistakably Grettir. Her face, accurately carved, bore a fearsome countenance. In her upraised hand she wielded a tiny pyramid, ready to strike.

"Behold," said Mälar, nudging the pile with his toe.

Other idols, carved of ivory or soft stone or strange gray rock filled with tiny holes, bore the images of Northmen in full battle regalia. Their eyes and mouths were closed, as if they were sleeping, or dead.

"They knew we were coming and they feared Grettir greatly," said Mälar.

"Yes," Halberd replied. "They, too, regarded her as a witch. The Skrælings carried her likeness either to ward her off or to grant her the obeisance she demanded. The dead Northmen require little interpretation: either the Skrælings once worshiped them as foes of Grettir, or they are meant to represent our doom. Either way, these people wish no trade or treaty with us."

"Further," said Usuthu, joining them by the pile, "our men are terrified by the sight of themselves in this pile."

The crewmen stared anxiously at the images they had collected. Some threw the small statues onto the pile as if the mere touch of them were poison. Others clutched the idols tightly, scrutinizing every inch for some sign, some omen, some clue to the fate of the men who had inspired the dread carvings. Halberd knew they needed to be calmed.

"We have sailed farther than any Northman before us," he began quietly. "We have massacred the Heathman and split the Sea of Blackness in the dead of winter. Dragons we have slain and great storms survived. A fiendish host has attacked with a ferocity that our grandchildren will speak of by the fires, and yet we stand, whole and strong."

The crew gathered around him as he spoke.

"Naturally, savages make idols of that which is strange to them. My brother and his crew lived here for months. Is it so odd that the Skrælings should carve their likenesses? Remember too that no gods may stand in the face of ours, as our victory on this Plain of Death has shown. To fear the god of a man you have vanquished is foolishness. To fear the idol of another god is to blaspheme our own. Any of you who wish to renounce the gods of Aasgard may do so aloud and retain the Skræling idols to worship as you choose. Those who do not may now cast any idol onto the pile."

Every crewman shuffled his feet guiltily. Their fear of the Skrælings had subsided with victory. It had reappeared at the sight of themselves, carved in ivory and soft stone. They were fearful.

"The shaman speaks the truth when he invokes the power of Thor," said Gardar. "My fealty to him demands that I spurn any spoils from this fight." He tossed a handful of tiny statues onto the pile.

"But," he continued, "it is clear that Valdane's wife is far more potent than any of us dreamed. I will not live on this rock, under her power, until spring. I say this now clear and loudly, so that all will know that I remain loyal. When the ship is repaired, regardless of the season, I will leave."

The crew nodded solemnly. Halberd, long resigned to this new schedule, said nothing. Gardar beckoned to the crew.

They threw their idols onto the pile. The proportion of Northmen statues was disturbing. At least a quarter of the idols in the pile were representations of the Northmen or Grettir. The rest were strange sea creatures and land animals typical of the coldest climates.

Usuthu came forward with a battle-mallet in his hand. Modeled after the Hammer of Thor, it had a simple iron head with two flat striking surfaces bound to a stout handle with overlapping rawhide. Usuthu knelt over the pile. With one mighty swing he smashed half of the small figures into splinters.

The crew stepped back as tiny shards of ivory and stone whistled past. Usuthu kept his head down and his arm moving until all the idols were destroyed. Every member of the crew felt each loud crunch go through him like an arrow.

Usuthu gathered up the splinters and threw them into a waiting bonfire.

The Northmen watched the fire carefully. It was not always wise to so blatantly assault the power of the gods of strangers. Perhaps these gods would rise out of the fire and smite them.

Perhaps Grettir had not fled at all, but was hidden in one of these idols. Perhaps the fire would unleash her fury. In the cold night and leaping flames, with home unimaginable leagues away, anything seemed possible.

But the splinters of the gods melted without incident.

As the flames rose the sun fell from the sky. Cold set in, hard biting cold, undercut with a chill the Northmen had not felt at sea. They huddled around the fire and glanced up at the strange sky, which was filled with stars they had never seen. Off in the distance they heard the barklike shouts and grunting noises of a Skræling ceremony. No doubt the barbarians were mourning their dead while plotting a bloody revenge.

The fire burned down slowly, sinking into the snow. When only embers remained the Northmen stared into the pit of ash and snow. They were uncertain of their next step.

Halberd clapped his hands together to bring the blood back to his fingertips.

"To oars," he called. "We must move the *Freyja* up to the greathouse tonight, to give us cover against an attack tomorrow."

The crew groaned at the thought of hauling the ship so far in the dark, but none doubted the correctness of the strategy.

Soon the oars were in place and the *Freyja* moving smoothly up the hill. Though the night was pitch-black the hillside was smooth, frozen snow. It creaked loudly beneath the weight of the ship, but was neither slippery nor so soft that a man sank into it. The crew were glad for a task and soon were warm. Also banished by this chore was the fearsome lassitude which overcomes a man after he has lived through a battle. An army left to its own devices after such heavy bloodshed would soon be asleep where it stood.

Even so, the men were exhausted. They had been days at sea, spent the afternoon in battle and the evening hauling their boat. They were greatly relieved when they reached the crest of the rise on which the greathouse sat.

The *Freyja* slid the last few yards onto the level plain. Halberd, Gardar, Usuthu, and Mälar collapsed by her prow. The remaining crewmen sank onto the frozen snow next to their oars. The cold air was filled with the sound of their breathing.

"Tonight we make camp and eat our fill," said Mälar. "In all my days at sea never have I seen savages attack quickly after such heavy losses."

"They have much praying and weeping to do," agreed Gardar. "I know not whether they are demon or human, but they have lost many warriors. I think we need not fear them."

"We'll leave one man on watch," Halberd said flatly, in a voice of command. "They have retired to their village, if not to mourn then certainly to dine on Janor the Insane. His bleeding head will make them a fine meal."

"Do not be too pleased with the gift of your lives," said Mälar loudly, so that all the young crew might hear. "Our lack of vigilance cost us the finest helmsman I have ever seen. We must not let our guard down again. Now that we have achieved this snow-covered rock we must have fresh meat and water soon. Tomorrow we shall hunt. So, tonight we shall eat. Let us break out the stores and fill our bellies. Let every horn of mead be lifted in toast to Janor the Insane. He shall be missed."

Halberd looked to the old man with admiration and no small amount of shock. Mälar, despite his years, was not too vain to have learned the value of Janor the Insane. Mälar's kind words likely provided all the funeral Janor would ever have.

"And we must have fortification from the Skrælings." shouted Labrans. "We must get inside the greathouse and sleep behind its sturdy walls."

The crew, filled with thoughts of Janor, surprised by Labrans' loud tones and lack of reverence for the dead, stared at him blankly. For a moment, no one spoke.

"Indeed, Labrans," said Gardar, "your behavior grows odder and odder with every passing day. I worry for you. Have you been taken with fever?"

"Is it fever to wish to sleep protected?" Labrans spat, his eyes slitted in fury.

"No," answered Gardar, "but fever speaks for you now. Gaze upon this greathouse. The door is not open yet no one calls to us from inside. Is it deserted? Is it filled with our dead brothers? If they are all dead, who sealed this door and why? I'll not open it while the stars shine. Too many curses roam the Earth at night."

The crew eyed Labrans with suspicion. He

stared around the encircled crew, looking into each face for support. He found none.

After a few moments, Labrans rose unsteadily and lurched toward the wood-and-iron door of the stone greathouse.

"Hold, my brother," Halberd said wearily.

"Hold I shall not, little brother!" Labrans spat in reply. "Friends of mine, and my brother too, sailed to this rock and built this house. No sign of them have I seen, and I am sick at heart. I will open this house and learn what remains of them."

"Labrans, we are all tired," said Gardar. "Only ill fortune awaits us behind that door, and all know it. Let us sleep tonight and tomorrow we shall examine our fate."

Labran's eyes gleamed again with a strange light.

"I will open that door tonight!" He shouted. "I must know Valdane's fate." He drew his mace from his belt, more, it seemed, to beat down the door than to threaten his brother.

Usuthu stealthily nodded to Halberd.

Halberd said nothing. His crew were exhausted. They didn't seem to care one way or the other. The greathouse was a forbidding sight. Its great wood-and-iron door was larger than Usuthu. No windows broke its walls, only vertical slits from which to fire arrows. No light shone from within, and there was no sign of life. The younger crewmen, especially, did not much care to open such a place in the dead of night.

"Labrans, you are raving," said Thorsten flatly. He rested with the crew, their backs against the hull of the *Freyja*. "Let it go until morning. We would all sleep."

Labrans leaned against the door, which bore no handle or knob, and pushed with all his remaining strength. The door gave not an inch. Labrans raised his mace and struck the door a shattering blow.

A deep, gloomy boom echoed through the length of the greathouse. The door did not budge, but a small dent showed in the wood.

"Hold, you fool," spat Mälar. "Do you see wood nearby to rebuild such a door? How shall we stand off the Skrælings if you smash it in now?"

"Aye," said Gardar. "Rest your body and put your head to work. There might be foul spirits in that house, bound inside by the strength of the door. I will not welcome them at night, when they are strong and we are weak. Wait till the morrow, when sunlight gives us power."

As gently as he could, Halberd spoke. "Labrans, my brother, we all grieve as you do. However, none wishes that door open tonight but you, and you cannot open it alone. Let it be until morning, and then we shall know the truth."

"And if you will not let it be," said Gardar, "if you wish to risk my life and spirit with your impatience, then I say to you what your brother may not. To open that door, you must step over my body."

Gardar rose to his feet, showing no sign of fatigue. He pulled his sword from its scabbard. The blade scraped along its side.

"And mine," said Mälar. He slid to his feet like a lizard, his spear in his fist.

Labrans looked to his brother.

"You would allow servants to threaten your brother?" he demanded. "Do the ties of family mean nothing in this frozen land?"

"Labrans, my blood-brother," Halberd replied without excitement, "all these men are my family. I am responsible for their lives as I am my own. Nothing shall endanger our quest. I beg you to climb aboard the *Freyja* and find the peace of sleep. If you challenge these men I will not come to your aid. Nor will any other."

Labrans flung his mace to the ground. He stalked to the ship and swung himself aboard. The men could hear him grunting his way into his sleeping furs.

"A fine idea," said Mälar. "Jump to your furs. We four shall split the watch tonight, but I do not think the Skrælings will attack before morning, if then."

"Gardar," said Halberd, "You have done well tonight. Take the first watch. Stand just below the *Freyja* and wake me when the night is one-quarter through."

"I cannot read these stars, Halberd. How will I know the proper hour?"

"Wake me when you are sleepy then. Now go."

When the crew was sleeping in the *Freyja* and Gardar standing well below it, Halberd spoke with urgency to Mälar and Usuthu.

"I know that Labrans is slowly being possessed. The Jewel glows whenever he seeks to lead us. I fear that something inside the greathouse would bring us harm tonight."

"We must watch him carefully and never let

him lead the crew," said Mälar. "Not in hunting, not in battle, and never at sea."

"The crew does not want to obey him anyway," said Usuthu. "His spirit is strong, but his call for followers grates on the ears."

"Because we do not hear his voice," said Halberd. "We hear that of Grettir."

"What," asked Mälar, "is inside the greathouse?"

"I feel it strongly," said Usuthu. "Death, and that which is not yet dead."

"I am as near to death as I hope I shall come until it strikes me," said Halberd. "And I have the next watch. Tomorrow we shall open the house and more. Tomorrow we shall find my brother. Now, however, I shall sleep."

Kvasir's Ghost

Usuthu, who had the last watch, awakened Halberd before the rest of the crew. Leaving their sleeping furs, they moved around the *Freyja* and surveyed the land they had sailed so far to see. From their location atop the rise they could see for leagues in every direction.

Morning brought a flat gray sky and piercing light without sun. The *Freyja* rested atop the gentle hill with the stone greathouse behind her. To the west and north ran the snowy plain, running down to the cut and into the ice cliffs to the west, and after many leagues, merging with a thick forest of evergreen trees to the north.

To the south the plain ran into a wide expanse of black stones, the broad black beach which led down to the sea. This was not the open ocean, but a sea lagoon. The lagoon was more than a league wide. Bordering it, and protecting it from the open ocean, was a wall of ice.

From beyond the ice cliffs which defined the cut they could see plumes of smoke rising into the frigid morning air. The Skrælings camped there. The cliffs made an excellent fortress. From its heights the Skrælings could observe their every move, but they could not see the Skrælings.

"We have lost five of our crew, and now Janor," Halberd said quietly. "We must lose no more or the *Freyja* will lack crewmen for the return to Northland. We shall protect our crew and look to avoid any battles with the Skrælings."

"When the crew sails east in the *Freyja*," Usuthu asked, "how shall we continue west to the Unknown World?"

Halberd looked at his friend with admiration. Though he had known for some time that his crew would insist on returning home at the earliest possible moment, Halberd had never considered this course. Halberd was not certain Usuthu would be willing to sail the open ocean in a two-man craft. Halberd was prepared to offer Usuthu the chance to return home.

"I should have known," Halberd said, "that you alone would master your fear and want to continue our search."

"Your destiny and mine are linked," Usuthu replied. "I have never retreated from a challenge nor stopped short of my destiny. I will not do so now. Therefore, neither shall you."

"I do not know what craft we shall use," Halberd said. "Perhaps Mälar can make us a small boat before he sails east."

"Ah, but I shall not sail east, my freinds," said Mälar, startling them as he appeared around the corner of the *Freyja*'s stern. "I insist upon going as far west as one can go until the edge of the ocean rests against the Unknown World. I am old and this is my last adventure. I shall not see Northland again."

"What of a boat, then?"

"I have seen other savages in cold climates take to the open sea in large canoes of skin. I believe I can make one large enough for three."

"Perhaps you should construct it for four," said Halberd. "I cannot deny my brother, Labrans, a place in this adventure, and I fear he will demand to accompany us."

"If he is under Grettir's spell . . ." began Mälar.

"The easier it will be to learn her wiles and ways by observing him closely," Halberd said. "I cannot abandon my brother."

"Your loyalty may command a fearsome price, but I will not question it," said Mälar. "Now, let us rouse the crew."

With a small fire roaring and warm food inside them for the first time in days, the crew appeared rested and strong.

"My brother wishes to enter the greathouse," began Halberd. "Before we take this risk, and face whatever waits inside, there is much I would discuss."

"Gardar, you are now second in command below Mälar. I rely upon you and your oath to keep order."

"Second in command? And where will you be, if not here?"

"Usuthu and I must travel down to the Beach of Stones to find the bones of my brother. There I must dream. I will not return for several days. Mälar and Gardar, you shall lead an expedition to the forest to the north. Under Mälar's instruction the crew will hew trees to repair the ship and hunt for food and skins. Mälar must also build a large skin-canoe. The crew will do his bidding on this as well."

"And this canoe," asked Labrans, "will be used for what purpose?"

"To sail myself, Usuthu, and Mälar to the Unknown World."

A stunned silence reigned at the fire. Fear marked every crewman's face. No man had thought that Halberd would not return with them. Worse, they would be without the navigational services of Mälar. Who among them was up to the task of guiding the *Freyja* home?

"I'll not go east," Labrans declared, "when my brothers murderess roams to the West."

"I expected as much," Halberd replied. "There will be a place for you in my craft. Before we sail, however, you will swear before man and god that you will obey my commands."

"Swear I do, if my revenge depends upon it." Labrans sat and said nothing more.

Halberd and Usuthu exchanged worried looks. What revenge did Labrans mean? And against whom?

"Thorsten," said Mälar, "I choose you as my successor as ship's navigator. You will be relieved of all nighttime watches, so that you might study the stars under my tutelage. Further, I forbid you to stand in the front rank of any battle that may be joined while we remain on this pile of ice and rock. I will not lose nights of sleep only to find my pupil dead. All hear me! Should Thorsten pursue glory in battle it will serve only as proof of his cowardice toward the sea! No man may encourage him to put his body at risk nor mock him for guarding his life. This is my command."

Thorsten was chastened. He had not planned to repeat his reckless words of the night before. Mälar had not lived his many years without learning different and exotic ways of tearing the heads off his enemies. Now Thorsten's humiliation would come in a different form. He knew nothing of the stars and did not expect Mälar to be an understanding or compassionate teacher. Thorsten would have to work hard, though much glory could be his reward. Navigators on a par with Mälar were rare in all the World. If Thorsten learned well, he would be a sought-after man on any ship. Though young, he would be rich. Yet he would always owe the man he had felt was a mere old fool.

The crew nodded approvingly. It was sound policy. Only such an order would restrain one as hot-blooded as Thorsten. It appeared that Halberd and Mälar would not send them east without proper preparation. Although the crew were worried about sailing without their captain, they were relieved to know that they would soon go home.

"If we are to stay here long enough to repair the *Freyja* we must have shelter," Gardar said. "Though I would avoid it, I fear we must open the greathouse."

"How shall we breach the door?" Halberd asked.

"We cannot smash it down, but I believe I may force the lock."

"Go to, then."

Gardar knelt before the huge door. The crew clustered around behind him, all eyes glued to the keyhole. Behind them, Usuthu ignored the drama and kept watch for the Skrælings. Whatever lurked inside the dark stone house would not bother him. It's curse would be directed only at the Northmen. Bahaab Dahaabs had never let him fall prey to the spirits of others' gods. Men Usuthu might fear, if seldom, but spirits never.

Gardar ran the thin edge of his steel dagger into the lock and twisted carefully. The crew held their breath with each twist of his knife. The greathouse gave up no clues. No light came from within and no noise, save the unearthly echoing screech of Gardar's knifeblade against the metal lockbox.

Behind Gardar, the crew gripped their swords anxiously, twisting the handles back and forth in their hands. All knew weapons would be useless against the spirits, but none could break the habits of fear: when a man was afraid, he reached for his sword.

"Ah!" Gardar gasped.

Every crewman raised up on his toes for a better look.

The door swung open on silent leather hinges. Nothing was revealed. The inside of the greathouse was darker than any tomb.

The great dark door crashed into the wall on which it was mounted. As if triggered by the sound, a foul cloud rushed out of the house with the wind of a gale.

Gardar, kneeling most directly in its path, was

blasted aside like a leaf. He rolled on the frozen snow, clawing at his eyes, blood running from his nose.

Putrid, rotting flesh, month-old drying blood, ripped-open guts, and moldering wounds were borne on that wind. All the stench of a thousand open graves, swollen bodies gnawed by wolves and plundered by Dwarfs, ransacked by demons and crawling with maggots, poured over the Northmen and paralyzed them.

Five of the younger crewmen were on their hands and knees, spewing their breakfasts over their feet in great hacking coughs. Those not standing firm when the door was opened were blown over by the force of the wind. The death-laden gale tore weapons out of hands and blew helmets off of heads.

Halberd stood firm in the face of the wind, his hair blowing behind him. He held his sword before him with both hands, the Jewel of Kyrwyn-Coyne glowing like a coal. Though the Jewel forced the wind to part and go around him, the stench of death soaked into his clothes. Usuthu turned toward the force of the gale and held one huge hand up into its path.

"Split before my hand, spawn of Wotan!" he commanded. "Blow your curse not upon any who worship Bahaab Dahaabs! No breath of this wind shall touch my soul nor any demon borne upon it enter my spirit!"

Obligingly, the wind parted and not a breeze ruffled the Mongol shaman.

The wind stopped. No figure emerged from the greathouse. The crew gathered themselves.

Mälar rose from the snow, avoiding a large puddle of half-digested food.

"That breakfast had a fine flavor going down," he cried, "But not so pleasant a taste on the way up. Still, no man of the sea is a man if he cannot bear the same meal twice in a day."

"Silence, you fool!" barked Labrans. "We must see what demons drove this wind upon us." Labrans stepped toward the open door.

"I shall not be called a fool nor allow you to free spirits meant to be chained!" Mälar shouted.

He reached up and seized Labrans by the back of his leather armor. Yanking with all his might, he flung Labrans to the snow in a clatter of arms and leather.

Labrans started to his feet, sword in hand, but Mälar shuffled toward him and kicked him under the chin. Labrans flipped over and hit the snow with a thud. He did not move.

"That man is possessed, I hereby declare," shouted Mälar. "Obey no orders from him nor challenges accept. Feed and protect him as one of us, but do not follow his counsel in any matter."

Mälar looked to Halberd for support.

"Yes," said the shaman. "I believe some foul force inhabits my brother. Watch over him, but listen to him not."

"Must we bind him, then?" asked Thorsten.

"No, leave him armed and treat him as you would any man. I fear for his life if we admit our suspicions aloud. The demon inside him may abandon his body if it is no longer of use. Never let him be aware of this, but have one man guard him at all times."

Halberd and Usuthu moved to the door of the greathouse. They could see nothing. Why had Labrans rushed forward? Did he have a curse prepared, the shouting of which might unleash all within?

"Bring a torch," Halberd commanded quietly.

One was quickly placed on his hand.

Halberd crossed the threshold.

The floor was littered with rotting bodies. Every dead Northman had been torn open, as if by beasts. Every man's organs were gone from his chest and every face had the eyes plucked out. Every head had been lopped open at the hairline and the brains removed. The sightless, empty heads lolled on the floor, at the opposite end of the greathouse from their mangled bodies. Between the heads and the bodies lay all the weapons that had once belonged to the brave warriors who had been so horribly slain.

Curiously, there was no blood splashed on the greathouse floor, no stains of it on the walls.

Usuthu and Halberd stepped into the darkest corner of the greathouse, and there, huddled against the wall, were the ghosts and spirits of every dead body on the floor.

"Speak!" demanded Halberd, in the Language of the Dead. "It is I, Halberd, shaman of your village and brother of your leader, who command you."

The shifting spirits gazed back at Halberd with an odd look of hope.

"Have you come to send us to Aasgard?" one asked, the low tones of its speech whooshing through the greathouse and out the door. It was a dim pale outline of a man, a transparent tracing of a Northman warrior, clad in his armor, his beard full and his hair long. Through him Halberd could see the stones of the greathouse wall. Huddled around him, floating up into the eaves of the corner, were at least twenty more spirits, all Northmen.

"Yes, if you will tell me how you came to be slain."

"Beware Grettir, the Skræling witch. She has our blood in a cask, every drop, mixed with her spittle. She uses it to make warriors who cannot be slain."

"Is she still on this island?" asked Halberd, his bones chilling at the sight of this many dead still lingering on the Earth. Inside his head his teeth knocked softly together. Beside him, Usuthu made not a sound.

"No," the spirit whispered into his beard. "She has fled months before."

"How has she slain so many strong warriors?"

"She learned the language of the Skrælings. We had trade with them, for skins and skin-canoes and for food from the sea. She learned to control their demons and they became her slaves. Once she had enslaved the Skræling demons she found it easy to enslave the barbarians themselves.

"We did not try to stop her. We thought they worshiped her as a goddess for her fair hair, which they had never seen. We did not know her evil purpose, nor the extent of her knowledge. We laughed at the Skrælings for their obedience to her. It was to our purpose to have the Skrælings as our serfs. We were fools.

"When, far too late to save us, we gained some understanding of her power, we feared her as did the Skrælings. Over the protests of your brother, we banished her to the northern forest. We thought she had to be near to harm us. We never understood the full strength of her dark magic.

"One night, via a spell, she unbarred the door to the Skrælings while she slept many leagues away. She set them upon us. I do not know if they wished to fight us, but fight they did. When we gained some advantage in these close quarters she sent the Dwarves, Fjalar and Suttung, two of the fiendish warriors who battle our gods from their fortress in the middle world between Aasgard and Niflheim, and serve at the whim of Hel, to assist the Skrælings. How Grettir summoned them from Midgard I do not know.

"After we were slain, the Dwarves collected our blood, our eyes, and our organs. Wherever she may be, she sees with our eyes whatever these useless corpses might see. She therefore knows you are here."

"She knows all the same, my brother," replied Halberd. "Why do none of the others speak?"

"Because," answered the pathetic ghost, "Grettir returned when the battle was lost and tore out tongues from our mouths, so that none could spread the word of her treachery to the ravens of Odin. Likewise she stole the brains from our heads and boiled them into a soup. Much cunning in war did she and Fjalar attain from that brew.

"Myself, I suffered a wound in battle that

caused my body to lose all feeling. My limbs would not answer me and all my joints were frozen. They could not open my jaws to tear out my tongue and so left it behind in my skull."

"What is your wish, then?" asked Halberd. Silent tears rolled down his cheeks. Grettir's teachery had wiped out the finest warriors of his village. Many months had their souls suffered, locked in this greathouse with their plundered bodies.

"Burn these bodies. Give us proper burial and at least we may leave her clutches. Whether we fought bravely enough in the face of treachery to be taken to Aasgard we do not know. But Niflheim can hold no place worse than this."

"And," Halberd asked, choking on his tears. "what of my brother, Valdane?"

"Valdane slew many Skrælings in the doorway. When they could not get past his sword, Grettir sent the Dwarves into this greathouse directly from the Midgard, the Spirit World. They hacked him from behind with their axes. He lured both of them out to thc Beach of Stones while we dealt with the host of Skrælings. Valdane struck the head from Suttung and gutted him from nape to crotch, but Fjalar was more cunning and dealt your brother the deathblow. Valdane had led them to the beach to give us a better chance. He knew we might defeat the Skrælings by themselves, but never when they fought in league with the Dwarves.

"Valdane knew his life was forfeit when he engaged the Dwarves alone. His plan was sound, but no mortal could slay both of them. We could give him no aid. We were greatly outnumbered."

"If the Skrælings defeated you, here in your fortress"— Usuthu spoke for the first time—"why do they fear us in open battle?"

"Who is this black giant?" asked the ghost. "Is he your ally in a battle with the Dwarves?"

"No," said Halberd. "He is my brother under the skin. We fight together. He is a powerful shaman in his own land."

"Well, you shall need all the magic you may muster to defeat this witch. I hope he is as strong as he is large."

"What," demanded Halberd, of the Skrælings' apparent fear of us?"

"As I lay on this floor, my life draining into the great cask of the Dwarves, Grettir addressed the Skræling chiefs before she fled. Your sister-in-law told the Skrælings that you were the Underworld incarnate. She told them they must slay every one of you. If they did not, she said, you would leave no woman or child alive. Further, she told them that if they did not slay you to the last man, she would return to wreak terrible vengeance upon them.

"Grettir erred when she showed the Skrælings how much she feared you. They believe you are demons even more terrible than she. They fear you also have learned their spells, and that if they draw near enough to hear your words, you will enslave them."

"I have but one more question," said Halberd, "before I free your bodies from this torment."

"Your questions are no burden to me," the

spirit answered. "I have not spoken to man nor demon nor ghost in all the months since my death. If I have knowledge that may help you slay this witch and cut out her heart, ask me questions until my body has rotted away."

"Why did my brother wish to open this greathouse last night?"

"Ah . . . her final treachery. The witch holds our bodies under a spell, and none of us can discern how to break it. At night our bodies rise from the floor and bear their weapons, seeking some enemy to slay. Headless, they prance about the greathouse and practice their sword-thrusts and ax-blows upon one another. Perhaps you are the enemy for whom they wait. Perhaps if the door was opened at night, our headless corpses would be set upon you."

"Brave Northman, what was your name?"

"I was Kvasir, from the village near the sea, Jotun. I leave no family to grieve. I have always been a warrior, and death by sword is what I sought."

"You will have your place in Aasgard. I shall burn your bodies and free your spirits now."

"Leave the weapons from that pile," said Kvasir's ghost. "They are cursed and obey only Grettir."

"I will have vengeance, Kvasir. For you, for Valdane, and for myself."

"If you can, young shaman, you shall," the ghost answered. "I hope for your sake that you may, for if you do not, your fate will doubtless be worse than mine. Many times on that gruesome night of battle, she invoked your name. She hates you above all mortals."

Halberd and Usuthu turned to the door. Crammed into the doorway were the crew, Mälar at the forefront.

"How much did they hear?" asked Halberd.

"They heard much, but understood nothing. You were speaking a tongue none but shamans know."

"It is doubless better that they know as little as possible." Halberd replied. "Make a pyre in this room and set it ablaze. Do not let the men touch the weapons or the bodies."

"If we burn the house," called Gardar, "what will we use for shelter against attack?"

"The roof and door and hideous cargo here will burn, but not the stone walls. We may put up another roof with ease. Hurry and burn it now, while the short daylight lingers."

"What will we use for wood?"

"Tear the decking off the *Freyja*, you child!" shouted Mälar. "When we go to the woods we can find deck wood galore. If you take the deck from her center it will not damage her structure. Now, fill this horrid chamber and burn it out."

The men climbed into the *Freyja* and tore out her decks with their axes. Wood was handed down in a line and stacked in the center of the floor. The Northmen stepped over the rancid bodies with care. Though many had been to war for years and were accustomed to ruined corpses, none had seen the dead attacked with such ferocity.

Halberd, Usuthu, Mälar, and Gardar stood in

the greathouse, breathing shallowly through their mouths to avoid the stench, stacking the wood. They built the pyre over the mound of torn bodies to ensure that they would burn.

"What of the heads?" asked Gardar.

"Fling a few boards over them and make the blaze high enough to catch the entire inside of the house," said Mälar. "Once the house is burning we will throw on more boards to keep the flames high. Flesh is weak. It will melt."

The pyre grew until it reached over their heads. The spirits huddled in the corner, gazing at the boards with anticipation. They had been brave men, and deserved a better fate. At worst, thought Halberd, they would be sent to Midgard, to dwell with the Dwarves and Giants. After a millenium, if they proved their bravery in combat there, they might be permitted into Aasgard. None, he believed, would have to suffer under the rule of Hel, in Niflheim.

"How fares the daylight?" Halberd called to the men in the *Freyja*.

"Twilight falls and quickly," came the reply.

"Truly we are farther north than we have ever been," said Halberd. "The sun has remained in the sky no more than a few hours."

"Why do we care when the sun sets?" asked Mälar. "Are we ready for sleep again so soon?"

"When darkness comes, old man," said Usuthu, "these torn corpses will rise, under a sorceress' spell, seize their weapons, and attack us without mercy. What say you to that?"

"Thorsten!" shouted Mälar. "Bring me a torch! Now!"

As Labrans lingered in the doorway, gazing almost wistfully at the damage inside, Thorsten pushed him aside, bearing a torch. Mälar glanced at Halberd as he leaned toward the pyre.

"Do you wish to pray over these dead men and trapped souls, young sharman?" he asked.

"Yes, I pray that Grettir lives until I can cut out her heart. Now burn this house."

Halberd made for the door. Labrans was now leaning up against an inside wall. Halberd seized his arm and thrust him out the doorway. Usuthu followed the brothers. Mälar dropped his torch onto the pyre and jumped backward out the door.

The wood caught instantly. The flame raced up the pyre, ignited the beams which held up the roof and the wooden shingles of the roof itself. In a moment, the greathouse blazed along its length. The sun set slowly and twilight lingered, the broad, flat sky turning red from the sun, the roiling black smoke of the greathouse roof lying across the red sky like a giant black finger in the still air.

The pyre was swiftly consumed and the flames reached downward, searching for more fuel. The spirits made no sound. Their bodies, however, rose from the floor as the sun set, pushing aside the burning beams and struggling to reach their melting weapons. One headless, blazing corpse stumbled to the greathouse doorway, where a waiting Gardar pushed it back inside with the narrow end of an oar. The crew watched breathlessly over his shoulder. None had ever fought a dead man. None, including Halberd, knew how to kill one.

When two or three bodies had reached their feet, and seemed determined to gain the doorway, a fortuitous crack sounded from overhead. The roof, supported by beams now burned through, collapsed onto the pyre with a deafening whoosh. The flame, covered for a moment, burst forth even stronger, sending blue-yellow tentacles higher than the walls of the greathouse. Where once had rested a roof of shingles and thatch there now glowed a roof of flame.

The bodies inside were consumed by fire. The spirits were set free.

The stench of burning flesh carried over the heads of the men, down to the ice cliffs and into the camp of the Skrælings. What they would make of it, Halberd could not decide. They had shown no interest in attacking today. If their behavior held true to that of other savages, they would grieve for days to come and attack again when they felt their strength renewed. If he was to find Valdane and lose himself in dreams, he must do so swiftly. Halberd gestured to bring Gardar and Mälar close to him.

"When the fire has burned down to ashes, throw on more wood to burn even those embers down once again. Dig a pit for the ashes and have only Thorsten and Bjarni carry the ashes to it. They are too young and brave to be corrupted by any spells in the burned flesh. Cover the pit well and scrub down the walls of ashes before you clean the greathouse. Cover the burned floor with earth, not snow, and pile it deep. When it is covered, place a broadsword into it, point downward. Use any man's sword but Labrans', no matter what he says. Keep him on watch or with those in the forest. Do not let him plant his sword in the earthen floor. Do not even allow him to sleep in the greathouse. Use whatever ruse you must, but do not speak your intentions outright."

Halberd then addressed his crew. "I take my leave of you now. Mälar is your captain and Gardar is his second. I will return within four days."

"And if you do not?" The mocking voice could have come only from Labrans.

"Then sail the *Freyja* home and reclaim your gold from Lif."

Halberd reached into the *Freyja* and removed a skin bag holding food, water, arrows, and his sleeping furs. He looped this bag over his shoulder and set off down the gentle hill. Usuthu walked beside him.

The Beach of Stones

The darkness had no effect on their footing. The smooth hillside stretched on a gentle grade down to the sea. The moon would not be out tonight, nor would the stars, but the low clouds reflected the light off the snow and made their way easy.

Neither was concerned over the Skrælings. No matter how long the winter nights, savages in northern lands did not venture forth. Perhaps too many things, mortal or immortal, which liked to eat them prowled the frozen snow. Every savage tribe created its own reasons for staying indoors. They invented spirits in their minds that became so real they sprang to life in the Known World. Halberd had learned from Thessah how much evil had been brought into the Known World simply through the power of the imagination. Demons which tribes required, for whatever reason, soon walked the Earth.

After silent trudging for many minutes, Halberd heard the gentle sound of the sea upon the rocks.

"The snow ends here," Usuthu said.

Before them lay the broad black beach of stones. Every rock was flat and wide. The smallest was as large as a man's chest, the biggest almost the size of a pony. The sea slid over the rocks in gentle waves and fell into the channels between. The rocks were slick and glowed in the reflected light, ghostly and beckoning.

"If we do not slip and break our backs, we should find my brother without incident," Halberd said. He balanced his bag over his shoulder carefully and slid his ax out of its holster. "I do not want to have to reach for a weapon on this surface. One hard yank would send me flying. If evil comes, let us be ready."

Usuthu, who had dangled his fighting hammer from his wrist since they had landed, said nothing. Gingerly, they moved over the stones. They strongly felt the presence of magic, good and evil. It was a ghostly time. The rocks gleamed in the reflected light, the phosphorescence of the sea threw sparks over their feet as they walked, the darkness grew deeper.

It was only early afternoon. Spirits would be about in all lands at this time of day. Here they would be very strong, drawn by the blood, the death, the power of Grettir and the violent thoroughness of her treachery. Demons fed on the evil which she created, and her power would generate many offspring. Some had to be near.

After hours of careful stepping and sliding, leaping from rock to rock and fighting for balance as the waves splashed over their feet, Halberd saw a huddled form. On the rocks around it lay a shield, a helmet, and a broken sword.

"There, Usuthu, lies my brother."

Halberd could be patient no longer. He bounded

from one stone to the next, fighting for balance with every landing, pausing just long enough to shift his weight and gather himself for another slippery leap. Finally he stood over Valdane.

The scavenger animals had not been kind to his flesh, nor had the elements. His head had been scoured clean, picked of skin, eyes, hair, and brains. His skull rested on the black stones, bent forward in submission. His cloak and iron armor hung on a meatless skeleton, as did his fur leggings and boots. One hand was gone from the end of a bony arm, carried off by carrion eaters, either human animal, or demonic. His leather armor had been eaten away by sea creatures, tiny black spiderlike scuttling beasts which scurried away with a soft clacking sound at Halberd's approach. The impenetrable wood-and-iron door of the greathouse had protected the flesh of Kvasir and his warriors. Valdane had been left exposed.

Jutting up from the middle of his broken spine, still trapped in his bones, was the long pyramid knife. Halberd stood over Valdane's bones, waiting for Usuthu. When he heard the Mongol's step on the rock nearest him, he turned.

"Brother, do I pluck forth this knife?"

"The witch showed it to you, and left it for you to find. It holds sorcery of some kind, of that there is no doubt."

"True, but have it I must. It slew my brother. Perhaps it will slay her."

Halberd leaned over and gently pulled on the stone knife. Though held only by bone, it was stuck fast. Halberd laid his ax on the wet rock, knelt beside his brother, and pulled again. His knees slipped on the slick stone. Again, the pyramid held.

Halberd had no choice. To retrieve the knife he would have to take the stance that Grettir had held when she slew Valdane. No doubt this was her intention. Halberd gingerly straddled his brother's skeleton. Bracing with his feet on the slimy surface, he gripped the knife with both hands and drew on the haft steadily. Slowly, the stone pyramid came free.

When Halberd pulled out the knife, Valdane's skeleton collapsed onto the wet rock. His bony arms reached in front of him and his legs stretched behind. His skull rolled free of his neck and bounced into a crack between two stones. It rotated as it fell, and the empty eye sockets stared back at Halberd as the sea hissed into them and out again.

Halberd stood up, holding the knife in one hand. He felt a momentary enchantment, as if his body were alive with new powers and strength. The knife vibrated in his hand. Halberd looked to Usuthu, who nodded at Halberd's sword. Clearly the Jewel was aglow.

"This knife must open portals to other worlds," Halberd exclaimed. "But if Grettir wielded it, could it be benign?"

"Her strength lies only in evil," Usuthu answered." Use this knife with caution. The mere handling of it might enslave you. Test it before you claim it as your own."

"Already I feel new powers coursing through me. I must beware. Take the knife and tell me the effect it has upon you."

Usuthu gripped the pyramid. He stood even taller for a moment.

"I do not know if it is evil, but it is stronger than any object I have ever beheld. If she left such an implement behind it must perform some task no other force could accomplish."

"But what?"

At these words, Valdane's spirit slowly rose from his skeleton.

Like Kvasir, his spirit was a transparent replica of the man. Still, Valdane's ghost stood strong and tall and held its hands toward its brother. Its ghostly form opened its mouth to speak, but no sounds emerged. It extended its wispy arms to embrace Halberd, but they slipped past him, leaving only a cold, burning wind.

Halberd cried as he beheld what remained of his brother. As tears spurted from his eyes, a rumbling sounded up and down the rocky beach.

"Take this blade, brother," Usuthu whispered urgently. "It was meant for your hands and you must wield it now to save us."

Usuthu thrust the knife into Halberd's right hand. In the same motion he stooped to the rocks and scooped up Halberd's ax. This he pushed into Halberd's left hand. Halberd, stricken with grief, let his arms hang limp at his sides. The rumbling grew louder.

"Make yourself ready, brother," Usuthu hissed, pulling his curved sword from its scabbard. Halberd gazed at Valdane's spirit, dumbly. Valdane's ghost looked back at him, its face beaming with love. It too ignored the rumbling. Usuthu seized his friend by the shoulder with one great black hand and shook him roughly.

"Awake! If you are truly a warrior, then forget your grief and look to your vengeance!" Usuthu shouted, his voice echoing along the black stone beach. "The wall between the worlds cracks open in this place! Make you ready."

Usuthu dropped into his fighter's crouch, his curved sword held before him, scanning the horizon from side to side. In that instant Halberd realized how great was the danger he had invoked by freeing the trapped spirit of his brother. Valdane's ghost lost its smile of love and set its features into a hard, resigned stare. If worlds were colliding because it had emerged at last, its fate would not be pleasant.

The rumbling increased and the very Earth shook. As Halberd fought for balance, a Dwarf appeared before him, standing between him and the spirit of his dead brother.

Though all Giants were large, not all Dwarves were small. This one was huge: taller and stronger than Halberd, though smaller than Usuthu. His back was hunched and his hands enormous and powerful. His head was misshapen and bumpy. Tucked into his belt was a huge fighting ax, coated with dried blood and hair. He had a giant pig's snout, two beady eyes, and a mouth full of fangs. Spittle dropped from his teeth and sizzled when it hit the moist rocks at his gnarled and webbed feet. Sparse hairs sprouted from the top of his wart-covered skull and did a poor job of hiding two small flesh-colored horns. His tongue was tiny and forked, and leaped about his mouth as he spoke.

"Behold, mortal, I am Thund, come for this pathetic ghost. I am to bear him to Niflheim, there to serve Hel for all eternity."

"Why must my brother answer to Hel? Why is he not borne to Midgard? He was betrayed and is therefore denied Aasgard, but what crime tenders him to your care?"

"No crime, you little fool, but a bargain. Grettir the Witch has consigned him to Hel in exchange for certain favors. A warrior of his prowess will aid us greatly in our wars with the gods."

"Are you truly a Dwarf?" asked Halberd. "You appear great and strong. Are you in fact a Giant, here on some ruse? Or are you Loki, the Shape-Changer, in disguise, or even perhaps Odin, God of Gods?"

"Silence! I am merely Thund, but Thund is more than enough for you and your black giant. I have powers as no other Dwarf. These strengths are gifts from Hel. I sit on her right hand and she relies on me as no other. Now, I go."

Thund produced a slender golden chain from his leather chest armor and secured it around the neck of Valdane's ghost.

"Hold, please, oh wise and powerful Dwarf," Halberd pleaded. "We two are mere mortals and cannot resist you. But please, for the sake of mercy, let my brother speak to me."

The Dwarf preened a bit at Halberd's fawning tone, but his smile turned to a dripping leer.

"Do not speak to me of mercy—there is none in Niflheim. As for speech, what trickery do you attempt? Your brother's ghost has forfeited that power. The witch cut out his tongue before she finished him. Without a tongue, no man may speak, no spirit either."

"Then, foul beast," Halberd shouted, "give him the loan of yours!"

Halberd slammed the stone pyramid deep into the Dwarf's muscled chest. The knife slashed through Thund's leather armor as if it were butter. It hesitated as it struck bone and then gristle, but Halberd leaned on the haft and the stone sank to the Dwarf's heart, freezing him where he stood. Green, bilelike blood ran slowly from the wound and boiled up around the protruding haft of the pyramid.

"By the power of this knife, I command that your tongue shall be the instrument of my brother's speech! You shall stay and do my bidding until his tale is told and I have freed you."

Thund's beady little eyes rolled slowly backward in his skull. Only the bloodshot, yellowy whites were visible. His hands opened at his side and the golden chain tinkled off the rocks at his feet. His breathing was slow and regular.

"How did you know to do this?" asked Usuthu. "How could you know he would do your bidding?"

"I knew nothing and thought less, my brother," confessed Halberd. "I lost my reason at the sight of this monster and wished only to make him my slave."

"That you have achieved. Now let us hear from the ghost while this beast is stilled."

"Speak, my brother," Halberd implored the

ghost. Halberd could hardly believe what he had done. The knife had awesome power.

"We may not hold this Dwarf too long," cautioned Usuthu. "Hel will notice him missing and send others after him. Her temper will be aroused."

"So, you must speak to us now," Halberd said. "And tell us how your life was lost."

The ghost glided toward Halberd, but could not go around the Dwarf. Apparently some spell held Thund between the brothers. The ghost opened its mouth and moved the stump of its tongue. Valdane's voice, strong and reassuring, issued from the Dwarf's foul mouth.

"Ah, little brother," Valdane's spirit said, "you have grown quickly and learned much since last I saw you. Your boldness has granted us a few minutes. I have great pride in you. I knew you would come to release my soul and pursue my revenge."

Halberd sank to his knees on the glistening rock, crying freely. The sound of his brother's voice filled him with overwhelming love and sadness. To hear it from the stinking, slimy hole in this evil Dwarf's face was too much to bear. The gods must be laughing at him how.

"Arise, brother. Do not cry. My life was taken months ago. That tragedy is past. My fate is sealed. This beast will take me to Niflheim and I shall have to offer counsel to Hel. This I can bear if I know the witch will be slain."

"I shall slay her," said Halberd, slowly rising and wiping away his tears. "I shall slay her and bear her heart to you, wherever you may be."

"I believe you will," said the ghost, raising its

arms as if to offer Halbred a hug. When it tried to reach out, the body of Thund prevented any contact.

"So be it," Valdane's deep voice boomed from the Dwarf's mouth. "Here I shall stand and tell my tale.

"Our passage to Vinland was neither easy nor hard. We sailed to fair weather and swung far north, to avoid the Heathland Isles. We encountered a few beasts of the sea, but they were more curious than threatening. I do not think we unsheathed an arrow or showed a sword until near to Vinland itself.

"My bride behaved oddly on the day we left. She wept on her sleeping furs and spurned my body on the first night. On the second she accepted me. Truly, we had been man and wife for years before our marriage, and this was the first time she had forbade me her body on her bed. She would not say why.

"When we entered the Great Open Ocean she spent much of her time under a deck canvas, casting spells and consulting runes. She would not tell me what demons or gods she seeked to contact. The change in her began as we neared this rock. Her eyes burned from within and her demeanor changed. Grettir was always strong, but now she was needlessly cruel. Short with the crew, short with me and, as the journey neared its end, threatening.

"She practiced with her sword upon the mast every day, and made my crewman fight with her mock duels, to increase her prowess still. She grew stronger as we grew tired. After all, she did not row, she did not haul upon the sail lines, she did not fight the tiller, and she alone had privacy when she slept.

"Near to Vinland, close enough to see the cliffs, we were set upon by Nidhogg himself. Hel's serpeant struck at the ship and tore off the stern, taking the rudder and three crewman. Boards flew into the sky and blood as well. The sea surged in over the ravaged boat. The ship turned to, lost and on the verge of swamping. We filled the serpent with arrows, but they had no effect. We had sailed without a shaman and knew no spells with which to subdue the beast.

"Yet, he did not seek to destroy us. He hung back, observing the craft and waiting for some sign. Half of us bailed out the surging sea and half hurled lances at the beast. The water was cold and tired us quickly. We were lost.

"Then Grettir clambered atop the dragonhead prow. Though the sea tossed the ship like a wood chip she stood without support, balancing atop the narrow dragonhead, her feet together. As she raised her arms above her head the wind blew like a gale. Her eyes glowed with fire and her hair fanned out behind her, rising in the wind like a flame. The wind molded her white dress to her slender body. Despite the danger, I believe that every man on board wanted to tear that dress from her body and ravage her on the deck boards.

"In that horrible moment, I knew she was no longer my wife. She had fulfilled her destiny. She was a witch.

"She spake to the beast in some tongue I have

never heard, no matter that I have sailed or ridden to every corner of the Known World. She beckoned to the serpent and it approached her. She whispered into its ear and caressed its neck as if it were a pony. Nidhogg nuzzled her in return, his steaming breath enveloping her and hiding her from our view. When next we saw her, Nidhogg had vanished. Grettir remained on the prow. When she lowered her arms the wind ceased and the swells dropped from the surface of the sea. The ocean became as glass. Nidhogg appeared behind us. He lowered his great head and raised our broken stern from the sea, resting it upon his forehead. Thus, he bore us to the entrance of the ice cliffs. From there we made our way.

"When Grettir climbed down from the prow her eyes now longer glowed. She saw me plainly, but as if from a great distance. She told me she was no longer my wife and would not share my bed. She said that Vinland held her destiny and powers beyond my imagining. In that, she was right.

"No member of the crew dared challenge her after this feat. We could not know if she would aid us with her magic or ruin us. We made our way into the cut and set the boat there to stay. Expeditions we made to the forest for wood and to this very beach for the rocks which formed the greathouse. Fall here is not harsh, and the game in the forest was plentiful.

"When the greathouse was half built we saw a strange sight. Emerging from the Great Open Ocean, coming into the cut and moving through this very lagoon, were many, many skin-canoes. So many that the sea appeared to be sown with charcoal. A host of savages, Skrælings, climbed from the canoes and made straight for the ice cliffs, where they established a village.

"We awaited their attack every day, and spent much men and material in preparation, but the assault we feared never came. Every day the Skræling men would take their skin-canoes to the sea, and every night return with many fish and large sea mammals. At night their village sounded with ceremonies and chantings. We were fearful, but they appeared to be men of the sea, nothing more.

"At Grettir's behest we placed one day, near to the entrance of their village, bolts of our cloth and pieces of our sail canvas. At the end of that day a long procession of Skræling men approached our greathouse. They carried no arms, and so we left ours and walked down the plain to meet them. They bore fish and meat and skins and even the unclad wooden frame of a skin-canoe. They wanted very much to trade with us.

"Grettir led our party to meet them. Their shaman, an old and wizened man, seemed to know her. They embraced. Though I cannot swear to it, I believe that they expected her. I believe she embodied the fulfillment of their prophecy. Grettir spent not another night in the greathouse.

"During our long first night of trading and feasting with the Skrælings she sat close by this old shaman and they signed to one another for hours on end. As the sun rose and the feast ended, they spoke aloud and she required sign language no longer. They understood one another perfectly. Grettir would neither translate their tongue for us nor report on how she had learned it. All of us sat around her, sign-speaking with these savages like oafs, while Gettir spoke as easily as a Skræling born. On parting, the old shaman offered her the knife with which she slew me and you subdued this Dwarf.

"She returned to the Skræling village with the savages, despite my command to the contrary. In the freezing dawn, she bared her breast to me before the crew and ordered me to strike her heart from her chest. She pulled my dagger from my sheath and put it in my hand. She pressed her naked breast against my blade, while the Northmen and the Skrælings observed, saying nothing. I could not slay her—my mind was filled only with my physical desire for her and admiration for her courage. I wanted her body at that moment as I never had. My hand dropped to my side.

"Many oceans had I sailed, many battles fought, and always at the front I rode. Never was I weak. Never. Until that day. I could not smite her, though I prayed not long after for a second opportunity. She laughed at me and turned away. She did not follow the Skrælings to their camp. She led them!

"Grettir remained in the Skræling camp for three days and nights. I longed to take a force of men and rub the camp off the face of Earth. My crew dissuaded me. She was not taken by force, she sought their company, my crew said, and they spoke truly. We were vastly outnumbered but we were Northmen. We would not shirk to fight a superior force. My men were not cowards, as their manner of dying later proved. But they would not lose their lives, they said, to gain back something which had not been stolen. Indeed, we had other tasks. We constructed the greathouse and began to store food for the winter. We learned the ways of the Skræling skin-canoe and hunted large sea mammals here in this lagoon.

"On the morning of the fourth day Grettir returned. Again she walked at the head of a large Skræling force. This time, they were armed. Grettir stopped just below the greathouse. She spoke to us like a queen, saying that the Skrælings were hers to command, and hence ours. She beckoned the men forward and they made camp around the greathouse. From that day forth, they were ever at our side.

"They did our hunting in the lagoon. They led us to the best game trails in the forest. They showed to us what plants might be eaten and which would kill. They carried for us around the camp. At all times they looked to Grettir for leadership. They sat at her feet by the campfire and told her long tales in their barking language. She spoke back to them and they understood her without effort. At night she slept apart from both camps, though many nights she spent here on the Beach of Stones, praying and casting spells by her fire. The Skrælings longed to touch her hair, and from this we discerned that they worshiped her for her fair skin.

"To me she would not speak or come near. She

gazed at me with loathing and contempt. When once I tried to strike her she cast a spell with one word and my hand passed through her without stopping. She laughed in my face. My heart was heavy. Until that instant I had not feared her. But here was plain proof. She was no longer human.

"I called my men from the forest and from the Beach of Stones. We prepared our bows and lances and swords. Armed to the teeth and determined, we banished her to the northern forest that night. The entire crew stood behind me, clad in their armor, hot with the longing to put a knife in the breast of every Skræling. If Grettir had commanded it, the Skrælings would have risen up against us, but they accepted my judgment without comment or unrest. Some of the barbarian warriors left with her. Some stayed and continued to act as our serfs around the camp.

"We did not see her for days. Even though we went to the forest on hunts and left her food and thick furs against the coming cold, she kept herself and her warriors hidden from us. My heart yearned for her every night when I lay in my furs, and I dreaded the coming of winter's darkness for the first time in my life. I knew she would have revenge against us, but I assumed it would be petty or mischievous. Again, I underestimated her power.

"After she had been banished for three weeks, on the night of the Winter Solstice, when the daylight is shortest and the dark greatest in length, she struck. We awakened to flames. Our ship, which we had left unguarded since our apparent peace with the Skrælings, burned from prow to stern. It was completely consumed in seconds.

"Before we had time to grasp this treachery, another followed. The Skræling force attacked us in our greathouse, while we struggled from our furs. Our sentries they slew with knives in silence, but this assault filled the black sky with screams. They poured in through the greathouse door, which Grettir unbolted with a spell, though she was hidden in the forest, leagues away. The door flew open with a crash and the demons were upon us.

"The greathouse floor was covered with a thick, low-lying fog. I believe Grettir sent that fog to confuse us, but it worked to our advantage. The Skrælings could not see through it to the floor, and so struck blindly at our sleeping furs. We crawled around in it in search of our weapons and hacked at them from below.

"They fought without bows. They loved to kill at close quarters. In that they resembled Northmen, but in that only. They stabbed us in our furs and drove our heads from our bodies with their long ivory knives as we sought to rise. Blood soaked the floor. I rose, sword in hand, and chopped my way to the door. Beside me came your brother, Mahvreeds the Cautious.

"He had long expected an attack, as he always expected the worst in any situation. Mahvreeds slept in his armor. This night it saved his life, but not for long. He held the doorway with me, firing arrows into the demons from scant feet away, and piercing the furs of any who ventured near. We never looked back into the greathouse.

Our work was on the snowy plain. We trusted the crew to deal with the host inside and to protect our backs.

"Our crew, those who were not slain in their furs, rose up and smote the Skrælings inside. They made short work of the demons, who had never seen broadswords in action, and who, I think, underestimated the number of them we might kill in so small a space with so fearsome a weapon.

"As the number of Skrælings in the greathouse dwindled we were joined at the door by two more warriors. They fired arrows and hurled lances over our shoulders and drove the Skrælings farther back. In truth, though I knew I had caused the loss of many men, I was filled with joy. After days and weeks of longing in my heart, here was an enemy I could smite, and freely. I could not bring myself to kill Grettir, so I took my measure against the demons. Every head I chopped off, every heart I ran through, I rejoiced. My soul felt freedom. I knew that I would slay the host of Skrælings, make for the forest, and slay the witch who set them upon us, as well. At that moment, lost in the glory of battle, I believed that her death would restore to my heart its balance.

"My joy at the fight, and my confidence, fed the hearts of my men. Singing their songs of blood and screaming their battle-cries, they slew the last of the Skrælings inside. Indeed, our bare feet splashed in puddles of their blood. We rearmed ourselves with their knives and lances. The demons outside hesitated to press their attack. At that instant Grettir's full powers were revealed. Through some vicious bargain, which now clearly included the sale of my spirit and soul, she contacted Hel and bade her send two Dwarves into the fray against us.

"My back was to the greathouse. I heard only the warning screams of my men. Before I could turn, a burning pain tore through my back. Over my shoulder I could see the head of a giant ax. The blade was driven deeply into me. I forced myself out the doorway. My men followed, to engage the host and escape the Dwarves. The Skrælings attacked in force and the two groups mingled in front of the greathouse door in bloody and horrible confusion.

"The Skræling charge overran my men and forced them back into the greathouse. The force of the battle swept past me. I called to the Dwarves and insulted them to their faces. I cursed them and dared them to fight me. My intention was to occupy them fully and give my crew a chance to live. I need not have bothered. They were sent from Niflheim only for me.

"Fjalar, whose ax I bore in my back, tore the head from Mavreeds with one twitch of his clawed hand. The bleeding head sailed far into the night sky. Both Dwarves turned to watch it sail. Blood was sport for them, and cruelty their only amusement. As they turned to behold the head, I made for the Beach of Stones. I drew them far from the greathouse. They pursued me without hurry. They knew I was slain. Indeed, the trail of my blood from the hill to this beach was thick and easy to follow.

"Just as I underestimated Grettir, so did

Suttung mistake my blood for death. When he approached me I was very much alive. Lying on the wet stones in pain, I waited until he was directly over me. Then I ran my dagger deep into his body, at the place where his legs join. He screamed as his green blood splashed over these stones. I struggled to my feet and split his body open with my broadsword. As I slew him, he vanished. I rested upon my sword. When I turned, Fjalar was before me.

"Him I slashed across the face, but he was swifter and stronger than any man or demon I had ever fought. He cut my legs out from under me and held me still. As I struggled, he reached his taloned hand into my mouth and tore out my tongue. The blood filled my throat and I thought I would choke on my own essence. Instead, the Dwarf turned me over so that my blood would drain onto the ground. He held me under his foot and waited.

"Then I was no longer on the ground. I was in the air, held above his head by his powerful arms. He flung me far through the air, till I landed on this spot. I flew at least one league in the air. The force with which I hit threw the ax from my back and broke most of my bones. I was helpless. Strangely, when I raised up my head, I beheld you, little brother. I did not know whether this was spell or entrancement. Was I gazing at you from Aasgard, or had you transported yourself to Vinland to aid your dying brother? I could not know. But see you I did, and my plea reached your ears.

"Then Grettir reappeared and I am slain."

The Dwarf shut his mouth. Spittle ran in long strings from either side of his horrible jaws. Behind him, Valdane's ghost seemed neither weary nor bitter. It gazed at Halberd with love.

"You have come," Valdane's voice issued from the Dwarf. "You have come and you will take my revenge."

Halberd could not respond. He knelt on the stones, sobbing for his lost brother. To hear so treacherous a tale broke his heart. To hear it from the mouth of this fiend of Hel seemed sufficient to break his spirit as well.

"We have come for no other purpose," said Usuthu. "We have thrown away everything in our lives for this quest, and we shall not rest until it is fulfilled. This I vow, and your brother vows as well."

"Rise, then, brother," spake the Dwarf. "I do not want your tears. I want your strength. Cry for me no longer. My tale is tragic, but no more than that of any warrior."

Halberd regained his feet. His chest was heavy with the terrible secret he carried. Halberd knew in his soul that his lust for Grettir had triggered a curse. No doubt this curse drove Grettir to the darkest magic. This magic had led, in turn, to the treachery which slew Valdane. Halberd drew in a ragged breath, with which to utter the hidden truth.

"Speak to me not," said his brother's ghost, through his hideous translator, "if you would tell me things I did not know when I lived. Death is death and cannot be undone. Do not torture yourself with any secrets you may carry. Cast them into the wind and burden neither of us with them."

"But . . ." Halberd began, "I must speak to you of . . ."

"No," replied his brother's ghost. "Speak to me of nothing, but hear me well. I believe that Grettir loved you more than she ever cared for me. I believe that she waited many years for you to fight me for her hand, and this you never did. I believe that her love, some years ago, turned to bitterness and hate and that this bitterness drove her into the dark arms of magic.

"Long, long before she left Northland had she been a witch. Long before. I believe she practiced the dark arts for years prior to our marriage. I believe she went to our mother for counsel for the blackest purposes. I say this to warn you. She despises you. She seeks to slay you and more. She brought the spectacle of my death into your dreams only to lure you into her hands. Do not rest, do not trust her, and do not show her the mercy of love, as I did.

"Now, I can speak no more. The hour is at hand. Free this Dwarf and I shall accept my eternity in Niflheim."

"No!" cried Halberd. "This further do I swear to you. You shall not dwell in the Underworld forever. I shall learn to travel there and I will bargain with Hel for your freedom. This day cannot come soon, but come it will"

"Swear not what you cannot achieve. If you save me from Hel, so be it. If you do not, there is no shame. Farewell, Usuthu. Farewell, Halberd, farewell, my brother."

The ghost moved farther behind the Dwarf. Halberd reached forward and plucked the knife from Thund's chest. The beady eyes rolled back down and the great fists opened and closed. Thund stood unmoving, eyeing Halberd greedily from head to toe.

"Young shaman," the beast said gloatingly, "you are cunning, but still mortal. Mortals are fools. I will punish your brother every day for this trickery, and one day I shall return and slay you, bit by bit. Then your flesh shall be sprinkled on my dinner. What day that is, I shall not say. Dread the very thought of me until then."

"Never shall you hold sway over me, Thund. Not by fear nor threat. If you wish one day to slay me, let that day be now!"

Enraged, Halberd swung his ax left-handed at the Dwarf. Thund, too stunned by this effrontery to move, took the blow where his thick neck joined his hump shoulders. The ghastly crunch drew his head from his neck and sent it flying. It bounced off the stones and rolled into a large crack.

Halberd stood appalled by his action. He had slain a Dwarf. Few mortals dared this course. The consequences would be dire. Halberd dared not breathe. Usuthu calmly put his curved sword back into its sheath and raised his small hammer over his head, ready to strike in any direction. Thund's body did not fall over. Nor did Valdane's ghost move. The wind had ceased. The whole Earth stood waiting.

Thund's arms stretched into the air, groping for his head. Thund's head, held fast in the crack as the sea splashed around it, called out to the body.

"Come to me," the Dwarf cried. "Quickly, before I drown."

Thund's body strode unerringly to his head and lifted it gently. Cradling the head under one arm, Thund's body turned to Halberd. His other arm reached to Halberd, the yellowed, clawlike nails on the end of the warty fingers clacking together.

"Ah, mortal, perhaps the Dwarves and Giants which roam the Known World are not so difficult to slay as I," the head said, grinning horribly. "In this unknown wilderness, where humans are few and demons many, the Dwarves possess great strength and greater cruelty."

"You have committed a grave error. You have underestimated me."

The hole in his armor leaked green blood from his chest. Thund appeared unhurt.

"If you had the knowledge you lack, you might have slain me with that potent knife. As little as you know, the knife might soon enslave you. Do not stand in the path of the will of Hel. Give me that blade to carry to her, as she bade."

"No force of darkness shall hold power over me. Ever," Halberd replied. "As for slaying you, the task is merely incomplete. Step near to me again, that I might hack your limbs from your torso as well as your head."

"Ah, you are brave as well as stupid," The Dwarf's head said, his eyes opening wide and rolling about. "Your death shall make much greater sport. And much more potent will be my power when I have consumed you. Look over your shoulder every day, little warrior, for I will be coming. Fear my wrath, and fear that of Hel, when she hears how you have defiled her messenger and refused her request."

The Dwarf's head crackled with glee.

"No!" shouted Usuthu.

He swung his tiny hammer about his head and crashed it into the rock upon which Thund's body stood. Lightning shot from the sky and struck the rock. Tiny snakelike beams ran up Thund's legs and froze him where he stood, sparks shooting off his horns. Thunder boomed overhead and the blue-white electricity of the captured lightning bathed Halberd's startled face.

"Bahaab Dahaabs, enter this brutal world through your servant, Usuthu," the Mongol intoned. "Place your power in my hands and send a message to this demon and his keeper."

Usuthu held his hands at shoulder height, palms facing one another. Lightning leaped back and forth between them until it formed a racing, crackling hoop. Usuthu held the spinning hoop of energy over Thund's head. When Usuthu took his hands away the enchanted circle spun about the Dwarf's ears like a misplaced halo.

"Wear this until you see your mistress in the Underworld, and then speak this message as I speak it to you," Usuthu commanded the Dwarf in a singsong voice. "Oh mighty Hel, daughter of Loki, ruler of Niflheim, know that we two mortals mean you no disrespect. We have no quarrel with you, for no wise man would dare test your awesome anger.

"Know that your servant, this incompetent Dwarf, challenged us as warriors, men of honor. Know that we accepted his challenge and removed his head. Know too that Thund does not bear the stone knife to you. The pyramid is our trophy. With it, perhaps one day we may buy back from you that which Thund now transports."

Usuthu raised his small hammer another time, and smote the Dwarf viciously on the shoulder. Though Thund's severed head cried out in pain, his broken arm did not drop his head.

"I am offended that you would threaten my brother with revenge," Usuthu said. "What of me? Do you not wish vengeance on me as well? I too have insulted you, and am your master. Am I now not included in your plans? Speak in reply, hideous Evil, I command you!"

"Yes," Thund's head whispered, its beady eyes burning with hate, "I shall have your flesh for breakfast and your black skin to wear as my cloak. Your head shall stay attached to your skin, living and feeling the pain of being flayed, for all eternity."

"Then, truly," Usuthu laughed, "my head shall prove more cunning than your own, which is already parted from its lonely shoulders. Now, take your poor treasure and begone. You are still under my spell, and this, also, I command."

The Dwarf turned back to Valdane's ghost, which had not moved. Thund picked up the slender golden chain in his free hand and looped it over the neck of the ghost. Lightly tugging on the chain, Thund drew the ghost near.

"Farewell, brother," Halberd called. "We shall see you again in this lifetime. This I swear."

The Dwarf faced Halberd and Usuthu. The crown of lightning spun around his heads, throwing tiny sparks and crackling loudly.

"Break this enchantment for a moment, that I might speak freely," Thund begged, through teeth gritted in pain.

"Begone, worm, you are defeated," Usuthu snapped, waving one hand dismissively.

Thund, and the helpless spirit of Halberd's brother, vanished.

The Plain of Death

When Halberd and Usuthu trudged up the last of the hill before the greathouse, only Thorsten remained on guard. It was the morning after they had heard the words of Valdane's ghost. They had rested for some time, and in their exhaustion the entire night had been required for the walk back.

"Where are the others?" Halberd wearily greeted Thorsten.

"They have gone to the forest for logs and skins. They will return in one more day."

"You are alone?"

"In this world I am alone, but the spirits surround me."

"What of the Skrælings?"

"There is no sign of them. The village makes no noise or smoke, and tracks of many warriors lead to the great forest. Mälar believes that they follow the main force of Northmen and fear this greathouse."

The Skrælings could be preparing for a mass attack far from the stronghold of the greathouse. Perhaps they were spying on the Northmen for

Grettir, and would report to her in some supernatural way.

"And you, Thorsten, do you fear the greathouse?"

"I dare not sleep inside. I sleep in the *Freyja*, as do most of the crew."

"Who among you is brave enough to face the spirits?"

"Only Mälar. But he sleeps there not."

"And why?"

"When it became known that fear would keep all awake but himself, Labrans demanded to accompany him. Mälar then ruled that no one could pass the night inside until your safe return."

"I shall sleep there now. I must dream for our future."

Halberd dropped his bag by the doorway and stepped inside. There was as yet no roof, but the blackened spars had been removed. The stone walls were washed clean. No trace of ash or soot. The dirt floor was thick and level. In its middle a broadsword staked the Northmen's claim. Twin serpents of gold and silver formed its handle. The finely wrought snakes gleamed as a shaft of morning light fell upon them through the empty roof.

"Thorsten, whose sword protects this place?" Halberd called out the doorless doorway.

"Mälar's," came the short reply.

"And what does your new captain use as a weapon?"

"He has bade Labrans swear an oath to be his strong right arm. Labrans must protect Mälar's life even at the risk of his own."

"And has Labrans served faithfully?"

"Truly and well."

Mälar was a cunning old dog. Labrans' loyalty to such an oath should outweigh the demonic force of any spell. If Labrans served without dishonor, then the power of the spell which bound him could be lessened. Labrans could be Halberd's true brother once more. This solved the problem of keeping watch on Labrans. He was, in effect, keeping watch on himself. Further, unless the spell-weaver wished Labrans' possession to become obvious, Labrans would have to be allowed to protect Mälar. Mälar clearly believed that he was alert enough to know when he might be jeopardy from Labrans.

Halberd dragged his sleeping fur into the darkest corner of the greathouse. He had no need to caution Usuthu. The Mongol would let no others inside while he dreamed.

As they stumbled back from the beach, they had talked of Usuthu's great power.

"Whence comes this hammer, Usuthu? I am almost afraid. Is it Mjollnar in some other form?"

"I have never heard that name."

"Mjollnar is the hammer of Thor. Thor wields it to establish order, to fight the Giants and Dwarves and to bear him through the air rapidly. His hammer resembles this one."

"This mallet has followed the line of sons in my family for over one thousand years. It is one of the most sacred and famous weapons on the Steppes. Much blood has flowed over the centuries to keep it in my family, though I am sure they attained it by theft. My father handed it down to me prior to our journey to the Blue River."

"Why did you not smash my head in, when we struggled in the forest?"

"To use it against a mortal would be to abuse its great strength. Also, I had no time to reach for it. Hence, I have worn it on my wrist since we landed. If I require it, I shall not want for it.

"Tell me," Usuthu continued, "What course do you believe Thund will pursue?"

Halberd answered rapidly, for he had been studying that question since they had vanquished the Dwarf.

"First, he will be severely chastised by Hel, for we have made a fool of him. Then he must work sorcerer's magic to secure his head to his shoulders. Between punishment and healing he should be unable to leave Niflheim for some days. Hel I do not fear now more than I have ever feared her. We have made our obeisance to her, we have expressed our dread and respect. If she is as spiteful as her father, Loki, then we are doomed. Yet I believe she will find only amusement at the plight of her Dwarf. I am hopeful this will cause her to respect us in return. Of Valdane I will not allow myself to think.

"As for Thund, he will come to us in some terrible form, animal or human. He will not show himself plainly. When his revenge is manifest, his power will be awesome to behold."

"Then to be ready for him," said Usuthu, "you must learn the way of the knife."

The quest for that knowledge brought Halberd to the greathouse, sleeping fur in hand. Only in the Dream World would he come to understand the knife. He took one grave risk, however. Grettir knew the Dream World and bent it to her will. She moved in it as she pleased and Halberd could not gauge the extent of her powers there. He could, however, accurately assess his own: they were, at best, limited. In time he would understand the Dream World, perhaps even master it. Now he had reason to fear Grettir. If she caught him there, where her powers were extensive and his just emerging, she might slay him fearfully. From Fallat he had learned that death in one World meant instant death in the other.

Halberd had no choice. Knowledge was never gained without sacrifice.

Wearily Halberd stripped off his leather armor. As they had spoken, Usuthu had sewn a new leather pouch to hold the pyramid knife. Hanging from the back, just below his heart, the knife was concealed from prying eyes, but was easily gained by either hand. The holster rested between his shoulders, near the center of his back. Halberd's three-sided stabbing dagger still hung in its horizontal sheath just above his waist. The placement of the new pouch would not interfere with his sword-stroke.

Halberd sat on his sleeping fur. He drank deeply from a skin of water and quickly choked down the cooked meat of some game animal. Halberd lacked appetite, but he knew he must be strong for this dream. It might last for days. He climbed into his furs, clutched the pyramid to his chest, slid his broadsword into the bag beside him, that he might awake and see the Jewel of Kyrwyn-Coyne, and fell instantly asleep.

Halberd flies over the green landscape once again. His heart fills with the peace and contentment his earlier dreams brought him. He sees the winding river below him and then endless green forests. He moves through the air without effort, without motion. His sword hangs at his side, and the pyramid knife rests in his hand.

He walks along a dappled forest path. The air is cool and still. Green leaves and broad branches break the sunlight into random patterns along the path. Many different birdsongs fill the air. It seems to be morning. Large horned game animals, such as he has never seen, stroll unafraid through the woods. They do not regard his presence as a threat.

"Have I died and been borne to the hunting lands of Aasgard?"

He walks for some time on this path, soaking up the warm sun and cool, crisp air, listening to the birds and gently shedding the tension of the previous weeks. For the first time since his dream of Valdane, Halberd is not weary.

Another bend of the path brings Halberd within sight of a strange village. The sunlight falls fully on the odd dwellings. They sit in a cluster by a gentle bend in the river, on a green hillside. There is a campfire with racks of drying fish and meat. Small children, brown and long-haired, who resemble the Skrælings of Vinland slightly, run and play among the dwellings.

The dwellings are made of painted skin, supported by tall poles to form a cone. Smoke drifts from the holes at the top of these cones. All is peaceful. Halberd's heart aches. He longs to run into the village. Though he has never seen or dreamed of this place, Halberd feels that he is welcome.

The flap at the round entrance to one of these dwelling cones is flung aside. The lovely, black-haired, black-eyed Skræling woman from his earlier dreams steps out. At the sight of Halberd she smiles. Her eyes fill with tears and her face is alight with joy.

She is tall and strong. Her black hair falls down her back in two thick braids. Her eyes are as black as her hair and they glow with love. She moves gracefully, and wears a long, supple deerskin dress, decorated with hundreds of brightly colored quills of a sort Halberd has never seen. She resembles the Skrælings, with their broad cheekbones and dignified faces, but her eyes are almond-shaped, not slits, and her cheekbones are sharp and defined, not flat. Their skin is yellow and hers is deep, lustrous brown, tinged slightly with red.

Halberd is smitten with a love he has never before felt, despite all his tortured longing and lust for Grettir. This love speaks of home and gentleness.

The woman waves a greeting. Halberd takes another step toward the village and it seems to recede, by the distance of one step.

"What treachery is this?" he cries. "Do not show me paradise only to remove it."

Halberd moves another step nearer and again

the village backs away. It seems the path lengthens as he draws nearer.

"Hold," calls the lovely woman. Finally, Halberd can hear her clearly. His heart pounds. He can barely draw the breath he needs.

"So," he gasps, "I hear and see you."

"Yes, brave warrior, for the first time, but not the last."

"Why does the village escape me? Why may I not come in?"

"You are too far from this village in the Waking World. When you draw nearer to the Unknown World you will find this place with ease. Further, this village is protected from all evil, therefore, none may enter who dare to hold Hrungnir."

Halberd's breath quickens yet again at the thought of learning the secret of the pyramid knife.

"You know this weapon then?" he asks.

"Yes, and too well," she replies. "Sorcery hath sprung Hrungnir from its home in Niflheim. It holds power over many creatures, some mortal and many who are not. Even in the Dream World we fear it. We do not permit it into our village, for its power is so great that any man, no matter how good, would harm another to own it."

"Why was it left for me to find, then? Who would willingly surrender such a force?"

"I have watched you for many weeks, since the day that Grettir the Witch invaded our world. At great price have I made myself knowledgeable in all events concerning you. Many days have I peered through the veil between our worlds, the better to observe your former love.

"I do not believe she left it for you. I believe the Dwarf, Thund, was meant to retrieve it before you found your brother. Though Grettir paid an awesome price for the Knife, Hel cheated her on the exchange. Grettir never used Hrurgnir as she might have. She does not appreciate its strength. She commanded that only the true guardian of Valdane's soul could yank Hrungnir from his fleshless bones.

"This guardian she did not name. She intended it to be Thund, but Thund is only a slave-bearer, a pathetic sentry. The true guardian of your brother's spirit is you. Once Grettir cast the spell over your brother's bones, only you, Halberd, could have plucked forth Hrungnir."

"But why should Hel want me to have Hrungnir?" Halberd asks the beautiful woman. "Thund is her servant. If Thund returns with both the Knife and Valdane, then Hel has cheated Grettir all around."

"Ah . . . Grettir attempted a bargain with Thund. She has promised the Dwarf to loose him upon the world, to free him from his service to Hel, if he returns Hrurgnir to her. Thund believes that Hel does not know of this bargain, but Hel knows, as she has always known much. She is the daughter of Loki, and Hrungnir was forged by him after all. Hel would not take the chance that Thund might turn on her, or that his power might be free to threaten man and gods. She therefore schemed upon Grettir's ignorance and was rewarded."

"Why did Grettir leave the knife in my brother's spine?"

"To own Valdane's soul, to keep it captive for delivery to Hel, Grettir must trap his spirit within his bleached and broken bones. Hrungnir was the only tool for the task."

"And now the Knife is mine."

"Yes."

"Is it purely evil, then? Am I now polluted by its power?"

"Hrungnir is merely strong, stronger than any single weapon mortals own. Such strength is seldom used for good. Such power has corrupted any mortal who wielded the Rock."

"Must I fear it?"

"No, you must guard it. If it will not be yours, then it will be Grettir's. You must guard the Knife from the witch, as you must guard yourself from the Knife."

"When may I enter your village?"

"When next you come, if you do not bear the Hrungnir."

"How then," Halberd demanded, "shall I protect myself from the witch, should she attack me in your world?"

"Her power in this World is fierce, yet she may not enter our village. When you draw nearer to us in the Waking World, your dreams will bear you straight to this spot. Once here, you need fear nothing."

"Why will I come?"

"Because I call you, and beckon you, and enchant you to be near me."

"And why?" Halberd asks, his pounding heart

and short breath, his overwhelming sense of space and safety, providing the answer before it was spoken.

"Because I am your lover, Halberd. Because I am your guide in this world. Because you will not travel in the Unknown World without me at your side."

"What are you called?"

"I am Ishlanawanda."

"Are you a sorceress?"

"I live in the Dream World," she answered simply. "I have powers here, to a degree. In the Waking World I have none. There I may not go. I may peer into it, I may watch as things occur, but I live in this World."

"How is it you have found me?"

"Our fates were ordained long ago. When Fallat, the evil shaman whose head you removed, was slain, there was much rejoicing.

"Fallat was the sole shaman powerful enough to venture into our world so far from his own. His power was terrifying. He could not penetrate the spell around our village, though he tried for centuries. With you, he made a fatal slip. He thought of you as a boy, an easy victim. Had he paid a bit more care, you would not be here today.

"From that episode you became known to me. Since then I have observed you, as best I could over the vast distance which separates us. I brought myself as near to you as my powers permitted. I could not see you clearly, nor you me, when so much of the earth lay between us.

What I have been able to see has only made my love for you increase.

"I could never show myself plainly to you until you drew nearer to my world. When you place one foot upon the soil of what you call the Unknown World, then may we touch."

"Aye. My love for you overwhelms me," Halberd interjected. "Your spirit inhabits me now, and grants me greater calmness than I have ever known.

"But, tell me," Halberd continues, "are you a Skræling? You resemble them in some way, though you are so lovely."

"All inhabitants of the Unknown World, Dreaming and Waking, are Skrælings. We are mem-bers of different tribes and have varying customs. We are all descendants of the same gods and mortals who walked in the Unknown World, both Dreaming and Waking, long ago. Some are more savage and some less so. The Skrælings on Vinland are fearsome indeed."

"Who are these gods, then? Does not Odin hold sway in this land?"

"No, Halberd. There are many gods in the Unknown World. Odin will watch you and rule you, as does Thor. But do not call upon them for help. They are strong, but seldom do they conflict with the gods of this land. You, Halberd, are the first of their servants ever to see it, save Grettir."

"Who dominates in the Unknown World?"

"Wonkan Tonca, the Grandfather, rules us all. The Four Winds answer to him, as do the spirits of all things. In the Unknown World, many things have souls which, in your world, are barren."

"How many I come to know the ways of the Skrælings, to speak to them as Grettir does, to know their gods and to answer their spells?"

"When you are able to come into my village, much may I teach you, but not before that day."

"You know much of this knife—now, what of the Jewel?" Halberd holds his sword in front of him, so Ishlanawanda may see the Jewel.

"It is older even than the Hrurgrir. None may speak to you of its power; that you must learn for yourself, as you must learn Hrungnir's. Thus far you have learned that it glows when you have entered my world. That is only a fraction of its power. Grettir fears the Jewel, perhaps as much as she fears the knife. Of this I may not say more."

"What becomes of my body in the Waking World, when I am here?"

"It is only asleep, vulnerable as you might be whenever you sleep. Similarly, when you visit my world, you must be on guard against all attacks. If you are slain here then you are slain."

"My heart is filled with love for you," Halberd speaks softly, "and glad I am that you have called to me, but I have duties to my crew, to my brother and to my quest, so that I may not remain. I will come to you in love and come to you for the aid which you have offered, but I cannot hide from the Waking World in the World of Dreams. It seems I am to be torn between the two."

"Would you hide here from that which you must achieve, then neither your lover nor your guide would I be. When you have crossed the sea, and step onto the Unknown World, come to me again. Farewell."

Ishlanawanda waves sadly, and turns back to her odd dwelling. She pulls aside the flap and disappears inside. Halberd sighs, his heart filling with joy, and turns back to the path.

Halberd left the path and entered the twi-light between dreaming and waking. He felt a mixture of joy and profound sadness. With his eyes still closed he began to rise from his furs when a potent force seized him by the shoulder and slammed him into his furs.

Instantly he was returned to the path in the forest.

Before him stands Grettir, her eyes ablaze, her hand outstretched.

"Nearer my trap have you come," she hisses, "but nearer still must you travel. My love is more jealous than you might imagine. I'll not lose you to any in this World or any other. When first you step upon the shores of the Unknown World, there shall I smite you, and there shall you perish, in body and in soul."

Grettir's skin gleams in the sunlight. Her hair hangs free about her head. Her eyes glow with evil, but, as always, Halberd is hypnotized by her beauty.

"Come here to me, Halberd," she murmurs, her voice a soft caress. "Come here to me, now. We may make love in the World of Dreams. I shall not harm you. I want you as you have always wanted me. Once is not enough for lust as strong as ours. Step nearer, and kiss me deeply."

Her final words float on the air like a butterfly. She reaches for Halberd, gently.

Despite his loathing, Halberd feels his manhood rise. The sight of her was as hypnotic as ever. His desire for Grettir, profane and damning, overtakes him once again. His heart pounds in his chest and his hands tremble. Clearly Halberd remembers the smooth feel of her flesh, the twisting heat of her passion and the soft words in his ear. Unable to resist, as if entranced, Halberd takes one step toward his sister-in-law, his lover, the Great Witch.

"Your powers are strong," he cries, "but I will not yield! I banish you from my dreams by the power of Hrungnir!"

Halberd snatches the pyramid from his belt and holds it before him. Grettir reaches for it instinctively, and then retreats a step, fear in her eyes.

"Ah, yes," she says in a voice as smooth as silk swapped from the traders from the Land of Sand, "Thund told me of your incredible find. But, my little lover, Hrungnir is not yours to command. It was meant for me and to me shall you return it. Bear it forward, and we shall spend the rest of our lives as lovers, here in this peaceful world."

Her eyes glow with love, and something darker. Her pink tongue traces the outline of her lips, while her hands mold her white witch's gown to her hips.

"Come, Halberd," Grettir moans, her voice husky, coming from deep in her throat, "give me Hrungnir, and be my love."

Again, despite his will, Halberd reaches out for a moment, the pyramid in hand, ready to do Grettir's bidding. With a gasp, he catches himself. Overhead, the sun hides behind black and threatening clouds. The Dream World shakes from their conflict. Halberd holds Hrungnir above his head.

"Did you not hear me, witch?" he demands. "Hrungnir is mine to command, and by its power I cast you out! Leave the World of my dreams. Never return so long as I bear Hrungnir."

In a crash of thunder, her mouth open, screaming in protest, Grettir vanishes.

Halberd awakes.

Halberd lay in the dark corner of the greathouse. He gripped the pyramid so tightly that blood ran down his hands from the cracked skin of his fingers. Usuthu sat next to him, his back against the stone wall of the greathouse. His eyes were glowing with humor.

"You were laughing and shouting," said Usuthu. "Then, you raised Hrungnir overhead and began to scream in a tongue I do not know."

Halberd, his face splitting with a foolish smile, told Usuthu everything which had occurred.

Then you shall not need a woman in this world, as one awaits you when you sleep," Usuthu said. "As for the pyramid, never put it aside. Sleep with it in your hand. There will be many attempts to snatch it from you."

"What is that ringing sound outside?"

"The axes of the crew. You have slept for two days and nights. In that time wood has been brought and chopped, and repairs made. For once this crew show much will and purpose. They are not anxious to linger."

Halberd climbed from his furs and gently made his way to the doorway. He was famished and weak.

The crew greeted him with enthusiasm. Only Mälar remained silent, wryly observing the young shaman and waiting for his response to their labors.

Halberd pulled himself over the gunwales of the *Freyja*. She was a new ship. The deck-boards were replaced and sanded smooth. A new mast towered over the ship, snugly resting in its socket. The rails were repaired, and a new row of shields hung over each side.

"We have no paint for them," said Mälar, "But we will stain them with animal fat and that should keep out the sea."

Beside the *Freyja* was a large pile of cut wood and a messy jumble of shavings and chopped pieces. The men, scattered about the ship rigging lines or rubbing in tallow, paused as Halberd inspected their work. Mälar, grinning hugely now, was obviously pleased.

Halberd swung down beside him and they walked a short distance from the crew.

"The Skrælings follow us to the woods every day and watch our camp there at night. When we return, they vanish. As we chop, so do they. We believe they are making more weapons. The game is plentiful. We are drying meat behind the greathouse and there will be sufficient stores for the crew."

"What of Thorsten? Will he be a navigator?"

"He is not so bright," replied the old sailor, "but he wants to be rich. So, he listens well. Once at sea I think he will suffice. Truly, I believe he will guide them near to home and they will follow the shore the rest of the way. After that, he will never lead a boat into the sea again. I am instructing him accordingly."

"And Labrans?"

"He has followed his oath scrupulously. Indeed, he is not a willing partner to his enchantment. He tries much too hard to protect me for this to be true. When the witch is slain he will be saved. Until then, sleep with one eye open."

"How many more days?"

"If the Skrælings let us be, I think one or two more. We must return to the forest for limber green trees with which to make our skin-canoe. We were waiting only for you."

The crew gathered their weapons and collected a bit of dried meat. Thorsten, as before, stayed at the greathouse, bidden to study the stars at Mälar's command. The track through the snowy plain was well worn. The snow was hard and smooth under their boots, and the sky remained low and gray. By dark they were encamped at the edge of the forest.

Three of the crew took their bows and melted away into the trees.

"They hunt the large animals at night," Mälar said. "They seem to be elk or deer of some kind. The meat is good and the skins tough."

"Will we use their skins on our canoe?"

"Certainly not! We must slay one or two of the sea mammals and use their skins."

The night passed uneventfully. All through the next day Halberd and Usuthu remained at the camp, helping Mälar twist young saplings into a curious, elongated grid. Though strong, the canoe frame was quite light, and could be easily transported by two men. Throughout their chores, Labrans lingered nearby, one hand on his sword haft, watching the woods for any threat to Mälar. His constant presence meant that Halberd could not share the secrets of his dream with Mälar.

As the afternoon slowly turned to dusk, a sentry came running to the fire.

"Thorsten is making his way across the snowy plain. He is running, though no one chases him."

"He has fled the greathouse," said Halberd. "I believe the spirits of those warriors have been released to their fates. Further, their bodies have been cleaved and burned, yet still I worry. Grettir's power is overwhelming. She may have some control over their very ashes we may not understand. If the sword is plucked from the floor, the spirits may rise and follow Grettir's bidding."

"Aye, and I'll have no sword," said Mälar. To the sentry he spoke quietly. "Tell the crew to stop their work and arm themselves. Have all men prepare to return to the greathouse. Gather food and tools. Send two men here to bear this canoe frame."

The crew quickly gathered themselves and

made for the edge of the forest. As they reached the snowy plain Thorsten reached them, breathless and excited.

"Give water to the messenger," Halberd commanded.

It was brought and Thorsten drank deeply before collapsing onto the snow.

"The Skrælings are massing," he gasped. "Skin-canoes by the dozen are coming up the cut and into the lagoon. The water was black with them. All bear men and all the men are armed. I lost count of the canoes at sixty. Their force is immense."

"Why come here to tell us?" demanded Mälar. "What now of the greathouse?"

"Their force has given the greathouse a wide berth," came the breathless reply. "They have swung around it and move in this direction. They are chanting and grunting most foully. They shake their lances and follow a shaman who beats a skin drum and wears the full skin of a white bear. He is a fearsome sight. Soon they are upon us. I precede them only shortly."

"You have done well," said Halberd. "Rest in the rear rank, for doubtless we shall need your sword arm."

"We cannot match a force of this size in the open plain," said Gardar. "We must melt into the woods and take them as they enter."

"They will not walk into such a trap," said Halberd. "They will encircle the woods and wait us out. So far we have been blessed by mild weather. If the sky produces snow, or the cold increases, and we were trapped in these woods?

We would lose half our men. No, we must make our way through them back to the greathouse."

"How do we defeat them?" Gardar asked. "They must number in the hundreds."

"We shall not," replied Halberd. "I shall."

He set off out of the trees and onto the plain. Usuthu walked beside him.

After trotting no more than a league they could see the Skræling army. They darkened the plain in a long, snaking line, shaking their lances and chanting in step. Though they were some distance away, their chants carried well in the cold, clear air. When they were less than a league from Halberd, the head of the line stopped.

The shaman turned around and addressed his force in a loud voice. When he was done, the line broke into many smaller fragments, as the Skrælings made their camp.

Halberd gave swift instruction.

"Prepare the edge of this wood not for siege, but as a base from which to attack. Tomorrow, and you shall know when the time is right, spring forth from these woods with all your strength. Use your bows wisely and at once. When all arrows are gone, charge them, and scream like the warriors we are."

"And where will you be?" cried Thorsten. "When we assault this host without our leaders?"

"Thorsten, you are a leader now," said Mälar, "and must think like one. All know where he will be, save you. Now prepare to sleep and leave the old men alone."

Halberd and Usuthu left the forest and trotted back out to their vantage point on the snowy plain. There they climbed into their furs and waited for dawn. Usuthu fell instantly asleep. Halberd studied the low clouds from his furs and thought of his new love, Ishlanawanda.

She waited for him in a land he must always visit, and never remain for long. She held many qualities which were new to him in women. Her kindness sprang not from weakness, but strength. Her desire for him was not based on his riches, for her life required none. She had picked him from all the Waking World, just as he was destined for her. Soon he would be near enough to her to take her in his arms. Then he would dream for days.

The dawn broke red and cold. Halberd's breath froze as it left his mouth. His limbs were slow to answer him. He pulled himself out of his furs and looked south, toward the Skræling host. Usuthu stood relaxed, watching the Skrælings, an arrrow already in his bow.

"Are you strong, my brother?" asked the Mongol. "Or did you dream of your dreams, and spend yourself into your furs?"

"I dreamed only of one Skræling head, rolling on the pure white snow, washing the snow with blood. Now, let us discover whose head that might be."

Halberd and Usuthu walked slowly across the snow. When they were within plain sight of the Skræling camp, they stood shoulder to shoulder and waited to be seen.

Shouts from sentries roused the slowly waking camp, and as dawn broke through the clouds, sending red and blue shafts of blinding light down to glare off the snow, a small group of Skrælings raced toward the warriors, waving their lances and chanting together.

Usuthu calmly took them down by arrow, one by one, until a dozen Skrælings twitched on the snow, all run completely through and pinned to the frozen crust. Halberd neither lifted a weapon nor moved in any way.

The shaman was now up and studying the two from a distance. After much deliberation, he waved two long lines of savages toward them. The Skrælings made two pincers and tried to encircle the warriors while running around them at full speed.

Usuthu turned with the movement of the lines, nailing one and then another, as Halberd passed him his massive arrows. When, startled by the carnage and unable to hold discipline, the Skrælings broke their pincers and charged as a group, Usuthu shot them through the throat and killed two or three with each arrow. The snow became littered with their twitching corpses. The charge was broken.

The Skræling shaman seemed finally to reach a conclusion. He strode alone to the center of the plain, halfway between the warriors and his demon host. Halberd did not move. Usuthu rested his bow on the snow and walked to the shaman, slowly and with grave dignity.

They faced one another no more than ten feet apart. The shaman commenced a long speech, barking and grunting as the clouds swept out of the sky and the bright blue sky was revealed for the first time since the Northmen had landed.

The glare from the snow hurt the eye, but the shaman ignored it. After his speech, the shaman held up one finger to Usuthu. The Mongol nodded.

The shaman turned back to his men and held but one finger aloft. The Skrælings murmured among themselves, each looking into the face of his neighbor.

Usuthu held up one finger to the shaman. He sliced across that finger with the edge of his other hand, as if that hand were a knife. As he cut across the finger, it fell over as if dead.

Usuthu swept his hand over the assembled Skræling army and thrust his hand toward the sea. In response, the shaman stuck one finger into his own mouth and chewed on it lustily.

Usuthu swung the tiny hammer out, and rested it in one massive palm. He kissed his other hand and pressed it to the hammer. He leaned toward the shaman and offered the hammer to him. Though he recoiled when the giant leaned over him, the shaman likewise kissed his own hand and pressed it to the hammer. Usuthu took the hammer back and nodded his head, once.

The shaman nodded and turned away.

His army awaited him on the crest of the snow-covered hill. Clad in furs and bearing ivory lances and knives, they stood impassively. Across from them stared the Northmen.

Swords ready, arrows nocked, axes gleaming in the sun, the Vikings, though outnumbered, did not fear their enemy. Great battles and adventure were the lifeblood of the Northmen. True, the younger warriors missed their homes and longed to see them once more, but had they sailed so far, fought so many demons and survived such hardship to settle down and become farmers? Never. They had sailed for glory and here it was, looking them in the face.

Good fortune to Halberd. But if he failed, woe to the Skræling host.

Usuthu strode back to Halberd.

"It is agreed," he said, gravely. "They will send out a champion."

"They must fear your bow greatly, to agree to champions when their numbers are so vast."

"Remember, they are savages. They would regret the loss of one life, and they have seen us kill dozens. Also, they must have one man who has never been defeated. In him their faith will overcome their intelligence. If you best him, they will leave this place."

"And if I do not?"

"Then, he says, they will eat us all."

"Do you believe him?"

"He swore upon the hammer," said Usuthu. "If he violates that oath, I may freely use the hammer against them, even though they are mortals."

"Can even that hammer defeat such an army, my brother?"

"No," replied the Mongol calmly. "But it can make the Earth open and swallow them. Now, make you ready."

Halberd tightened his leather chest armor and made sure his weapons were snug in their scabbards. His ax he took from his belt and held lightly in his hand.

"Do not make the mistake Fallat made with

you," said Usuthu. "Though this champion is savage, he is certain to be cunning. Kill him swiftly and let us go on about our day."

Usuthu touched the hammer lightly to Halberd's forehead. A thrill ran through Halberd. The merciless urge to destroy, the battle-urge of the Steppes, raced through him. He could taste the blood of his enemy in his mouth. He saw his guts spilled across the snow. He heard the death-rattle in his enemy's throat.

He was ready.

Halberd walked to where the two had parlayed and waited. His breath was even and regular. His ax felt weightless in his hand and alive.

The Skræling host moved alarmingly near to him, in one long grunting line. When they were just out of lance range they stopped. Their numbers lined the horizon. Too late, Halberd saw that the sun was behind them. He would have to start the fight with its rays burning into his eyes.

The shaman returned to the front of his long line. He roughly pulled two men aside, and through the gap they had made stepped their champion. He was yet the largest Skræling Halberd had seen, but that was not unexpected. The champion here would almost certainly be their strongest man. Strangely, though, this demon was even larger than Halberd. This was odd, since every other Skræling barely reached his chest.

Their champion had the large, flat head of the Skrælings. His nose was mashed and had been broken many times. His wild black hair blew around his head in the gentle breeze. His expression was demonic. Instead of the usual loose fur tunic, he wore only light fur leggings and a shirt of odd fabric, which glowed in the sunlight. His hands were huge and gnarled, and his shoulders immense with muscle.

The champion bore only two lances and a long ivory knife. He wore no shield. Halberd waited, certain the Skræling would salute him in some way before their fight to the death began.

He was wrong.

The Skræling ambled toward him, relaxed and unconcerned, until he was just within lance range. Then, without preamble, warning, or even raising the lance to his shoulder, he flung the long ivory spear at Halberd.

The lance flashed across the snow. Its speed was greater than an arrow fired from a bow. It was a white blur.

Halberd flung himself sideways. The lance, guided by some supernatural hand, followed his path and struck his ax squarely in the blade. The force of its strike tore the ax from Halberd's hand and, unbelievably, pierced the axblade and pinned it to the snow. Halberd wasted only one short tug on the ax to determine that it was stuck fast. Ivory had penetrated the finest steel.

No human hand could make such a thrust.

"So, you are a true demon," said Halberd calmly, circling the Skræling and whipping the broadsword from his shoulder scabbard. "I think I know your name. In fact, was not your head rolling on the stones scant days ago? And was not it cast there by my ax? This is greater luck than I might have imagined. Come near to me now, and I shall kill you like a man."

The Skræling took one more shuffling step toward Halberd, his remaining lance in his right hand, the long knife in his left. He feinted to the left and Halberd ducked down to follow the feint, his broadsword up and in front of him, the grip firmly held in both hands. With one more step, fast as a falcon, the demon lunged at Halberd and, in defiance of the ways of nature, was instantly upon him, right in his face. The savage had covered ten steps of ground in one blinding invisible bound.

The demon's lance was raised high over his head, and his knife thrust low, at Halberd's groin. Halberd, with no time to swing his sword, kicked at the knife hand and struck the savage on his wrist. The knife swung away, for an instant. Instead of leaning away from the attack, Halberd pushed himself inside the range of any lance thrust and smashed the Skræling in the face with the butt of his broadsword.

The Jewel of Kyrwyn-Coyne was held in a delicate-looking nest of silver. The slender twirls were far from delicate. Woven by the smiths on the Guardian Rock at the entrance to the Inland Sea, they were tougher than a war-ax. The thin edges cut slivers of flesh from the Skræling's face, and blood ran freely.

Halberd scuttled back from the demon, gathering his wits. The sun still glared into his eyes and he could not see the eyes of his opponent. Deprived of this vital clue, Halberd could not know when the man-beast might strike. Halberd continued to circle to his right, to put the sun behind himself, and into the eyes of the Skræling.

The demon touched his face with the back of his lance-hand and laughed. As his hand dropped from his face he fired his lance with one blinding flick of his wrist. It flew with inhuman speed. The ivory blade took Halberd in his leather armor and hurled him backward across the snow. The slender point ran through his armor, through his left shoulder, and out the back of his armor. It rammed into the snow and held Halberd there.

The Skræling leaped at him again, the knife upraised, moving as swiftly as a shadow. Halberd, calm despite his wound, thrust upward with his right hand as the savage leaped. The knife stopped within inches of Halberd's face. There was a ripping sound as Halberd's broadsword tore through fur and flesh and into organs. The demon stopped, transfixed, and backed slowly away from Halberd, the broadsword still deep within him.

Halberd released the sword and rolled away to his right. With a great heave he freed the blade from the ice and knelt, then raised himself to his feet. He took the handle of the lance with both hands and yanked it out. The pain threatened to still his wits. He could feel the blood flow down inside his armor.

Holding the lance, which was coated with his blood, Halberd looked to his enemy. The Skræling stood above him, no more than an arm's length away, smiling. Halberd stepped quickly around the savage, until the sun shone over his own shoulder. At last he could see the demon clearly.

Still smiling, the Skræling reached below his crotch and grabbed the razor-sharp blade by what little of its length remained outside him. Grinning fiercely now, he drew the blade out of himself and held it aloft. Pouring from his wound, trickling down the blade, was his hot blood.

It boiled onto the snow. It was bright green.

"So, Dwarf," said Halberd. "You are revealed. I thought your mistress would keep you in the Underworld longer, the better to box your ears for your clumsiness."

"Perhaps she does not know I am here, mortal," the Dwarf replied, gloating. "Perhaps I have slipped the bond of her punishment to slay you and regain Hrungnir. Then shall I be more powerful even than Hel."

Thund, still in the form of a Skræling, raised the sword blade to his mouth. Slowly, his eyes on Halberd all the while, he ran his forked tongue a foot out of his mouth and licked the green blood from the blade.

As he absorbed the taste of his own blood he shed the form of a Skræling and became revealed as the hideous Dwarf that he was.

Halberd wasted no time. As the Dwarf was changing form, Halberd snatched the dagger from the sheath along his back and hurled himself at Thund. He thrust the dagger into Thund's throat. It ran through his neck and green blood drenched them both. Gripping Thund by the shoulder with his weakened left hand, Halberd sawed into the Dwarf's throat, hoping to again tear his head off his shoulders.

The blood spurted without effect. Thund wrapped his arms around Halberd and gripped him to his chest.

"Now, upstart, shall I snap your spine in two, and eat you as you writhe along the snow?"

Thund crushed the breath from Halberd and shook him as a rat shakes a dog. The Dwarf's foul breath, stinking of souls tortured and the gnawed flesh of human corpses, scorched Halberd's face. Though his life was leaving him, his will remained strong. Reaching behind him with his left arm, which hung free outside the Dwarf's mighty limbs, he drew Hrurgnir from its secret holster. With what seemed his final breath, Halberd stabbed the pyramid deep into the Dwarf's back, straight into the middle of his ghastly hump. Hrungnir buried itself into the hump and blood gushed straight out around the haft, as if the Knife were a fountain.

Thund opened his mouth to scream, and the souls of those he had eaten rushed forth and shot into the sky. They left his mouth in the form of flame, and a pillar of fire reached into the sky above the dying Dwarf's head. The searing blast blinded Halberd and scorched the hair from his face. He fell backward onto the snow and crawled away from the Dwarf like a broken insect.

Thund was on his knees. His head was straight back, pointed at the merciless blue sky. A tongue of flame stood straight above him, searing his head and melting the flesh around his eyes. Thund still groped with both hands for the knife in his back. Halberd staggered to his feet and ran around the crippled Dwarf.

As Thund's hair began to burn and the flesh of his face ran down his neck and shoulders like rain, Halberd snatched Hrungnir from the hump.

Thund screamed and raised his arms to the heavens. Halberd took careful aim and drove the pyramid into Thund's hump a second time, pulling and cutting downward, opening a long gash in the Dwarf's back.

A second blast of fire, this one coal-black, poured out of the Dwarf, mixed with his green blood. From this gash escaped the ghosts of three immortals, all Giants, whom Thund had tricked and slain.

Their spirits hesitated over the crumpled body of the Dwarf and looked briefly at Halberd, who sat on the snow, exhausted, gazing with horror at this explosion of evil.

"When you have need of aid in the Underworld, mortal," said the largest of the Giants, "Call upon Ragnarok, or Urd or Ull. In return for our freedom from the Dwarf, we will do your bidding. Once."

The spirits vanished.

Thund fell onto his chest, his legs drumming on the snow. He appeared to be floating in a sea of his own blood. He gargled horribly and twitched along the length of his body. His melted head sank into the puddle of his green blood and was still.

Halberd had slain an immortal.

What the consequence would be he could not imagine.

He climbed to his feet once more, hugging his wounded shoulder with his good right hand, and staggered to the Dwarf. He pulled on Hrungnir, but it would not come free. With a sigh of exasperation Halberd flung himself into the puddle of blood. He braced both feet against Thund's back and pulled on the knife while pushing with his feet. It slowly drew free.

Halberd clambered to his feet, soaked in the blood of the Dwarf, and waved the knife over his head. At the signal, the Northmen burst from the trees, shouting their battle-cries and brandishing their swords. As they charged, the sky was filled with arrows from Usuthu's bow. The Skrælings broke rank and fled down the hill, screaming in terror in their barking tongue.

The End of Winter

No Skræling looked back at the attacking Northmen. The snow was littered with their lances and knives, dropped in their haste to escape. Their shaman, clad in his bearskin and weighted down by his drums, stood over the half-melted body of Thund, his grizzled old face giving no clues to his thoughts.

He did not seem to fear the Northmen, perhaps because Usuthu had vowed that only the champions would suffer, perhaps because he was too old and wise to fear anything. He watched carefully as Halberd shrugged out of his leather armor and inspected his shoulder. The shouting Northmen, hurling recovered Skræling lances into the backs of the fleeing demons, swept around Halberd, Usuthu, and the shaman without pause. Only Mälar, trailed by the watchful Labrans, stepped up to them and ignored the bloodfeast which trailed across the plain.

Mälar eyed the green blood and gashed hump. He shook his head.

"Young captain," he said, "you have either saved us or ensured our doom. If Hel loved this fiend we are done. If she knew of his treachery perhaps we may yet survive."

The shaman shook the bear skin away from his arms and gently reached toward Halberd's wound. Labrans drew his sword halfway from its scabbard and Labrans seized the old Skræling's arm, but Usuthu stood fast, his arms folded over his chest shield.

Halberd sat calmly. He allowed the old man to inspect his wound. The Shaman bade him sit on the snow. The demon wiseman placed both hands into the puddle of Thund's blood and rubbed it into the wound on Halberd's back. Halberd could feel the edges of the hole closing. The shaman rubbed more of the Dwarf's blood into the large hole in Halberd's upper chest. The gash instantly sealed, leaving only a star-shaped scar.

The shaman shook his white-fur sleeves back over his hands and, gesturing to the horizon, swept his hands over the forest, the snow plain, and the ice cliffs. They followed his hand, but could not see what he pointed at. As the old man pointed, there came a booming crack from the snow-clad mountains beyond the forest. It was like a clap of thunder, but driven from the earth, not the sky.

The shaman waggled one finger at the Northmen, pointed to the sea, and smiled broadly. He turned and slowly strode away, following the trail of dead Skrælings, which led all the way down to the ice cliffs.

"What means this old fool?" demanded Labrans.

"I suspect," said Mälar, "That he is urging us

to flee this rock. He seems to think it will collapse about our ears."

"If anyone knows," said Usuthu, "it is he. Let us not tarry but follow his sound advice at once."

"What did he say?" asked Labrans.

"He said we should follow the crew and prepare to leave."

Before the words were out of Halberd's mouth, half of the crew reappeared on the plain. Their eyes were glassy and their sword arms drenched in blood to the elbow. The carnage had been fearsome.

"Halberd, you must come quickly," said Thorsten. "The Skrælings are rushing into their skin-canoes and fleeing as if the World were about to end. Their fear of you is great."

"Perhaps their world is ending," said Mälar. "And we remain on it while they flee."

Another boom sounded from the hills. Below that sound, growing louder, was the unmistakable gurgle of rushing water.

"I hear a river now," said Gardar, who had joined them on the plain. "I have not heard a running river in these woods before. What does this portend?"

"Whatever it may portend," answered Halberd, snapping his leather armor into place and retrieving his various weapons, "we must make ourselves ready to follow the good example of the Skrælings. Take these men, Gardar, and gather all our provisions from the forest. Do not forget the frame of the canoe. Grab all that you may and move to the greathouse swiftly."

"Halberd," said Gardar, "this I shall do if you

answer one question for me. What has become of your beard?"

Halberd ran his hands over his cheeks. They were smooth and clean-shaven, as they had not been since he was a lad. His eyebrows also were to be gone, and his mustache as well.

"The Dwarf has fried them off, with his breath made of souls," Halberd answered.

"Well, at worst," said Mälar, "Thund has made you young again. Now we must make haste."

The three trotted across the plain, Usuthu clasping Halberd under his arm to give him added strength. When they had achieved the greathouse they beheld an amazing sight.

The cut was filled with canoes, so much so that no water could be seen. The Skrælings were paddling over one another in their haste to escape. Likewise the lagoon was black with the Skræling vessels. A line of the demons ran from the village hidden in the ice cliffs down to the cut. Every man, woman, and child was fleeing Vinland.

"They cannot be running from us," said Halberd. "We must flee, and quickly. If these savages take to the open sea unafraid, then the weather must be fair."

"We do not have the skins I require for the canoe," said Mälar. He turned to the crewmen who loaded food and skins of water onto the *Freyja*.

"Five of you," he ordered, "go into that cut and slay the Skrælings who sail in a total of three canoes. Cut the sea-mammal skins from the canoes carefully and bring them to me. Do not fear the other Skrælings. They will ignore you."

While Mälar led the crew as they fitted out the *Freyja* with her new mast, filled the seachests with food and furs, and loaded the weapon bags with captured Skræling lances, the crewmen took their bows and knives to the cut to obtain the skins.

When they returned, unharmed, and dragging the dripping skins up the hill from the cut, the other half of the crew trotted into camp bearing the meat they had slain in the forest, the furs from those beasts, and, between two men, the willowy frame of the canoe.

While Halberd watched from his pearch on the *Freyja*, Mälar stretched the skins about the frame, securing them with wooden pegs and madly sewing the skins together.

All the while, Thorsten spoke.

"The snow on all the mountains is melting at once. I have never seen the like. A river races through the forest and across the plain where, yesterday, none existed. The snow from the plain joins this river, and it grows and grows. It pours over the cliff walls in a fall near the mouth of the Open Ocean.

"Where the Skrælings pass below this fall most are swamped, and yet they continue to flee. Nothing will stop them."

"Thorsten, cease your mouth's flapping," barked Mälar. "Do you have the provisions laid by that I have commanded?"

"Yes."

"Then prepare them as I told you."

Thorsten pulled from the deck of the *Freyja* four odd oars. They were smaller than the oars of the *Freyja*, and they had blades on either end.

"These we grip in the middle," said Mälar, "and stroke to either side as we ride in the canoe."

He had finished his labor. The canoe was as long as three men. It had a pointed back and front, with a high prow and an upswept stern. Ranged with equal proportion were four holes in the top of the skin covering the frame, from the front to the back.

"We shall each sit in one of these openings," Mälar said with pride. "Our legs lie on the floor and we paddle with our arms well clear of the sides. I will take the rear, since I alone can navigate. Halberd will sit in front of me and Usuthu in front of him. Labrans shall have the bow."

All nodded. None said what all thought: with Labrans in the bow he could strike none of them from behind.

Usuthu, Halberd, Mälar, and Labrans tied their skin-bags of food, weapons, and furs to the outside of the canoe, careful to balance the weight on either side. Halberd had the use of his left arm as if it had never been wounded.

The new mast for the *Freyja* was raised in the socket and pulled upright. The new sail was hung from her crossbar and lines attached. The crew heaped their equipment aboard and waited for a command.

"Men, you have served me well," Halberd said. "None of you are cowards and all have seen things no Northman before you has survived. Now, we must part. Thorsten has been well taught and Gardar is a wise captain. Obey these two and you will safely see home once more.

"Sail far north and avoid the Heathmen. Make no foolish stops along the way in search of booty. Your only riches from this cruise will be the gold which Lif safeguards for you and the tales others will tell by the fire to your greater glory. Now, let us feast and sleep upon the land once last time, and in the morning we shall all be off."

They gathered outside the greathouse, which all still feared, and ate around a roaring blaze. The rushing sound of water grew ever louder and the thick swarm of fleeing Skrælings never abated.

As dusk settled in, lighting the clear and frozen sky blue-gold, a crewman screamed in alarm and raised one hand toward the snowy plain. All swiveled their heads from the fire and looked in horror.

The plain had disappeared. Racing over its flat surface was a vast lake of water. All snows had vanished, melted in a matter of hours. True, the Northmen had noticed the air was warmer, but it was still cold enough to freeze the breath. How could the snow be melting?

"That torrent will not pass us by," said Halberd, "We must make ready to leave this place tonight."

As he spoke, a deafening crack, followed instantly by a long crashing sound, filled the sky. The ground shook beneath their feet, so that every man was flung to the snow.

"Behold!" screamed Thorsten.

The ice cliffs were collapsing into the sea.

Slowly, they toppled over, leaning their tops far out over the cut, and then falling in huge ice blocks as their bottoms gave way. The echoing booms made it impossible to hear the screams of the trapped Skrælings. When the ice blocks hit, the resulting splash carried higher than the cliff tops had previously stood, hurling the skin-canoes far out into what remained of the snowy plain. There, the crumpled canoes were caught in the racing current and plunged back over the falling cliff walls, into the rapidly filling cut. All the Skrælings below the cliffs were crushed and drowned.

"The same occurs beyond the lagoon," Halberd shouted over the din, and all eyes swung farther to the south.

The ice cliffs no longer ringed the lagoon, and the Open Ocean rushed toward the shore, borne on monstrous swells, fed by giant floes of dirty ice. The floes were larger than the greathouse, and raced at the Beach of Stones at breakneck speed. The huge crests swept the Skrælings before them, tossing their canoes into the darkening sky, and pitching the fur-clad demons into the icy sea. While the Northmen watched, the Beach of Stones disappeared. The water raced onward, up the long gentle hill which led to the greathouse.

Simultaneously, the cut, filled with ice and destroyed because the walls which defined it had vanished, also met the Open Ocean and raced up the hill toward the Northmen. All atop the hill realized their danger at once.

"To the boats!" screamed Halberd. "We have moments to live!"

The crew leaped into the *Freyja*, which rested atop her oars. Gardar and Thorsten tried to pull the oars free in vain.

"What shall we do for oars?" yelled Gardar, over the crashing of the nearing waves.

"All crew out of the ship!" shouted Halberd. "All out, now!"

The crew climbed back over the new gunwales of the *Freyja*. The rushing sea was no less than one league away.

"All hands shove the *Freyja* off her oars," Halberd called. "And down the hill to the sea. Seize your oars as she clears them, and may Thor watch over you!"

The crew put their shoulders to the stern of their beloved ship. She slid easily off her oars, which were embedded in the snow. As the *Freyja* gained speed down the hill, every man grabbed an oar and raced after her. Gardar was the first aboard, leaping for her stern and clambering over. He hurled a line back over the stern for any stragglers. All the crew save one made the stern before the bow of the *Freyja* hit the raising sea. He was swept under the swells, and vanished.

The first waves lifted the *Freyja* high, but she slid down the back side and bobbed like a cork in the newly calmed water. As she slid, Halberd, Usuthu, Mälar, and Labrans stuck themselves into their holes in the top of the skin canoe.

Barely had they tucked their legs inside when the sea reached them and bore them aloft. They too rode over the first swell and settled, next to the *Freyja*, in a new-made lagoon.

"Throw us a line, you buffoon," Mälar ordered Thorsten. Quickly the dragon head ship and the Skræling skin-canoe were made fast to one another.

"All the cliffs have fallen," Mälar called to Gardar, who manned the helm. "So this sea will find its own level quietly now. There should be no more swells caused by debris falling from above."

"What has caused this enchantment, Halberd?" the new captain of the *Freyja* asked across scant yards of dirty seawater, as their crafts bobbed side by side under the darkening sky. "Why has this rock suddenly melted?"

"I believe," replied the shaman, "That the death of Thund meant the end of winter here. Perhaps Vinland has been held in a spell of Grettir's making since they first arrived, and now that power is broken."

Beside him, Usuthu nodded in agreement.

"When an immortal is slain," Halberd continued, "one cannot estimate what power may be made, undone, or set in motion. Here we have seen the work of three months of spring performed in less than a day. The Skrælings knew that his death would mean devastation. Hence they fled. The shaman warned us, but I could not discern his intent."

Beside them, in the now quiet sea, floated many Skræling corpses, shattered pieces of canoes, broken weapons, and skins of water.

"So," said Mälar, "we are well provisioned,

and both crafts have destinations to pursue. If we linger in this sea of corpses, we shall be set upon by an army of ghosts, or worse. We must make for the Open Ocean and leave this rock behind."

"What of your golden-handled sword, old man?" mocked Thorsten from the gunwale of the *Freyja*, as he looked down upon their fragile craft.

The crews of both ships looked back to the top of the rise, where the greathouse had stood. It was gone. Over it washed the tranquil surface of the just-made lagoon, littered with bodies and weapons of the Skrælings.

"Let's hope it remains on guard in the floor of the greathouse," the old sailor answered. "Or else that those spirits cannot swim. Just because they are covered with freezing water doesn't mean they have lost their power."

This sobering thought encouraged both crews to cut the line which held their boats together.

"But," Mälar continued, "I shall need a sword where I am bound, and you have them all around you. Cast your sword across the water to me now, Thorsten. This is my final command to you."

To the howling laughter of the crewmen, Thorsten unstrapped his broadsword from his waist and pitched it, in its ornate scabbard, across the brief space between the separating crafts. It hit the water next to the canoe on a flat side, soaking Mälar with its splash. He deftly grabbed it before it could sink.

"Now," cried Halberd, "to the sea."

The crewmen on the *Freyja* took to their oars,

and the four in the canoe raised their tiny double-bladed paddles. The *Freyja* moved smoothly away while the canoe pitched and trembled, going in small circles, as the Northmen and the Mongol quickly learned their new tools.

Above them, the stars filled the clear, black sky.

After a few minutes, the canoe righted itself and sped after the *Freyja*. Halberd was stunned by the deftness and speed of the little craft. Soon they were flashing into the wake of the larger ship, passing by giant ice floes and more Skræling bodies.

No cut remained. No more cliff walls stood and nothing that might distinguish the Open Ocean from the littered sea through which they paddled. After a quarter of the night had passed, however, the sea suddenly emptied of both bodies and ice. Behind them the water was littered. Before them lay only the empty nighttime horizon.

"Here we part, my brothers," called Halberd.

"Yes," echoed Mälar. "Your course is to the east for five days and nights, and then north by northeast until your dragonhead prow hits land. With any luck, that land will be Northland. Our course is simply west."

"How will you know where to go?" called Gardar.

"The Unknown World is vast," said Halberd. "We shall strike it where we may and find the trail of the witch. Doubtless it is well marked."

"You are a brave warrior, Halberd," said Gardar. "And your black giant is the finest archer I have yet beheld. Good fortune in your quest. I fear we shall never meet again."

"Doubtless you are correct, Gardar," answered Halberd. "Our fate lies in the Unknown World, and there we shall live out our lives. Go to my father and mother, and tell them of our adventures here. Give them my love and respect."

"That I shall, Halberd. Fare you well"

Gardar raised a hand to the canoe as the two ships drifted farther apart. All his crewmen did the same.

Halberd watched the *Freyja* with a heavy heart. She was his ship, commissioned by his determination and paid for with his father's gold. She had survived great dangers and now she would sail out of his life. Built for a crew of twenty, she looked a bit deserted and ridiculous with her crew of fourteen. Empty oar ports marked both her sides.

"Gardar," Halberd called over the widening gap between the boats, "I give the *Freyja* to the remaining crew, to be owned equally and shared so long as she may float, on the condition that one-tenth of all booty gained while sailing her be given to Danyeel."

"Agreed," came the faint response.

"Fare you well, Mälar," called Thorsten. "You are a wise old fool and a fine teacher."

"Stay off the rocks, Thorsten," Mälar replied. "Now we are gone."

Halberd and Usuthu raised a final hand in farewell to the *Freyja*. Mälar turned his back to his old ship and dug his paddle fiercely into the black sea. Labrans never looked back at his old shipmates nor made a sound. He paddled rhythmically, no doubt lost in the grip of the spell which bound him.

Halberd watched the *Freyja* row east as they paddled west, stealing brief looks over his shoulder between strokes. When he could no longer make out her sail or stern, Halberd could still see her glistening wake cutting a white path across the black water. But the moonless sky threw little light over the ocean, and soon the *Freyja* was gone.

They paddled west, following the commands of Mälar, who tried to make sense of the unfamiliar sky, and trusting to the current which had borne them to Vinland. Though none said it aloud, all felt that navigation was not important.

Grettir awaited them in the Unknown World. They knew in their bones that they would find her again, and soon. All felt aligned with their fate. Even Labrans, deep within the spell which held him, knew he sailed to a world unlike any he had seen. Even he was ready.

The night slowly faded and bright day followed, with a burning sun which leaped off the gentle seas and lanced into their eyes. The waves were no higher than those on a lake, and the paddling was easy work, much less taxing than rowing aboard the *Freyja*. All day they followed the sun, drinking from their skins of water and chewing on dried meat.

They saw no beasts of the sea and were harassed by no serpents. On this leg of their journey, their path was clear.

Halberd dozed that night, standing a brief watch

and then awakening Usuthu or Mälar. Labrans no longer spoke to them, and they let him be. He paddled steadily and never attempted to throw them off course or damage the boat. As long as one remained awake to watch him, they felt he was no danger until they were ashore.

In Halberd's dreams little occurred. He flew once again over the village of Ishlanawanda, but made no attempt to walk the path. He knew she awaited him, and he would see her soon. When he was awake, he let his mind stay empty and free, roaming through his memories and marshaling his spells and powers. Very very soon, he knew, he would need them all.

On the third day the sky lowered and a gentle rain began to fall. It was the sort of rain which portends a landfall. After a morning of rain they paddled into a fogbank. The world was reduced to a thick gray cloud, in which they could barely see one another. Their voices echoed in the gloom and they ceased paddling. They could steer no course now, and the current was all they needed.

They drifted without speaking all afternoon and into the night. They knew their destination was near. The fog cleared and the rain returned, this time a soaking, driving rain that offered less visibility than the fog. It rained all night, but Halberd managed to sleep despite his drenched furs.

The morning broke gray and damp. The thick, low clouds hung overhead, thick with water. For the moment, the rain stopped. Ahead of the canoe, less than a league away, was the ghostly shore Grettir had shown in Halberd's dream.

It was flat and unending, with no fjords or mountains. Green trees lined the shore right to the water's edge. There was no beach, and the ocean lapped at the red-dirt banks below the unbroken wall of trees, which ran from horizon to horizon, north to south.

Their paddles rested across the canoe as the Northmen and the Mongol rocked in the gentle swell, listening to the sea slap against the shore.

Somewhere in that ghostly forest, Grettir waited.

They had reached the Unknown World.

SIGNET (0451)

DISTANT REALMS

☐ **THE COPPER CROWN: The First Novel of *The Keltiad* by Patricia Kennealy.** When their powers of magic waned on ancient Earth, the Kelts and their allies fled the planet for the freedom of distant star realms. But the stars were home to two enemy star fleets mobilized for final, devastating war . . . "A gorgeous yarn!"—Anne McCaffrey.
(143949—$3.50)

☐ **THE THRONE OF SCONE: The Second Novel of *The Keltiad* by Patricia Kennealy.** Aeron, Queen of the Kelts, has fled to the stars on a desperate mission to find the fabled Thirteen Treasures of King Arthur, hidden for hundreds of years. But while she pursues her destiny, all the forces of Keltia are mobilizing for war. "Brilliant!"—Anne McCaffrey.
(148215—$3.50)

☐ **BORDERLAND edited by Terri Windling and Mark Arnold.** Between the mysterious Elflands and the magicless world are a wild Borderland and the ancient city of Bordertown. Here elves and humans mingle in an uneasy truce, and in the old, abandoned parts of the city, runaways gather, rock-and-roll clubs glitter and kids and bands clash in musical, magical rivalry. (141725—$2.95)*

☐ **GREYBEARD by Brian Aldiss.** Radiation was the executioner in a world where starvation was a way of life—where hostile armed camps, deadly diseases and mutant creatures ruled. But into this world came Greybeard—the last preserver in a world gone mad, fighting desperately to find and save the last, lost hope of humankind . . . "Top-flight adventure tale . . ."—August Derleth *The Capital Times*
(146611—$2.95)

Prices slightly higher in Canada

Buy them at your local bookstore or use coupon on next page for ordering.

SIGNET SCIENCE FICTION

THE FIERCE CHIEFS & FEUDING CLANS

of the *Horseclans* Series by Robert Adams

(0451)

☐ **HORSECLANS ODYSSEY (Horseclans #7).** Milo of Morai promises the clans a return to their legendary homeland, but first they must teach their enemies the price of harming any people of the clans . . . (124162—$2.95)

☐ **THE DEATH OF A LEGEND (Horseclans #8).** When they are driven into unfamiliar territory, Bili and his troops are spotted by half-human creatures. Will these eerie beings use their powers of illusion to send the troops to their doom? (129350—$2.95)*

☐ **THE WITCH GODDESS (Horseclans #9).** Stranded in a land peopled by cannibals and half-humans, Bili and his warriors must battle these savages, as well as the Witchmen, evil scientists led by Dr. Erica Arenstein. Fighting both these dangerous groups, even Bili's proven warriors may not long survive . . . (140273—$2.95)*

☐ **BILI THE AXE (Horseclans #10).** With the help of powerful inhuman allies, Prince Byruhn has persuaded Bili and his warriors to delay their return to Confederation lands and join in his campaign against the deadly invading army . . . but are Bili and Prince Byruhn galloping straight into a steel-bladed trap from which death is the only release? (129288—$2.95)*

☐ **CHAMPION OF THE LAST BATTLE (Horseclans #11).** The time has come at last for Bili and Prince Byruhn to rally their troops for the final defense of New Kuhmbuhluhn. But within the very castle grounds stalks a creature of nightmare, striking down the defenders one by one in a reign of bloody terror that may prove far more deadly than the enemy at their gates . . . (133048—$2.95)*

*Prices slightly higher in Canada

Buy them at your local bookstore or use coupon on next page for ordering.

SIGNET (0451)

Travels in Time and Space

☐ **CASTAWAYS IN TIME by Robert Adams.** It was a storm to end all storms, but when the clouds finally cleared, Bass Foster and his five unexpected house guests find they are no longer in twentieth-century America. Instead, they are thrust into a bloody English past never written about in any history books. . . . (140990—$2.95)

☐ **CASTAWAYS IN TIME #2: THE SEVEN MAGICAL JEWELS OF IRELAND by Robert Adams.** Drawn through a hole in time, twentieth-century American Bass Foster finds himself hailed as a noble warrior and chosen to command King Arthur's army. Now Bass must face the menace of an unknown enemy that seeks, not only overthrow Arthur's kindgom, but to conquer and enslave their whole world. . . . (133404—$2.95)

☐ **CASTAWAYS IN TIME #3 OF QUESTS AND KINGS by Robert Adams.** Bass Foster, one of King Arthur's most valued commanders, is given a seemingly impossible mission—to unite the warring kingdoms of Ireland under Arthur's loyal allies. But in Ireland waits both treacherous friends—and foes who could destroy them all. . . . (145747—$2.95)

☐ **GLIDE PATH by Arthur C. Clarke.** From the starfields of *2001* Clarke voyages back to the glide paths of Earth. From JCD headquarters to Moonbase and the stars is the journey of mankind, and Clarke remains the expert in evoking the excitement of discoveries past or those yet undreamed of in the mind of man. (145665—$3.50)

Prices slightly higher in Canada.

Buy them at your local bookstore or use this convenient coupon for ordering.

NEW AMERICAN LIBRARY
P.O. Box 999, Bergenfield, New Jersey 07621

Please send me the books I have checked above. I am enclosing $__________
(please add $1.00 to this order to cover postage and handling). Send check or money order—no cash or C.O.D.'s. Prices and numbers are subject to change without notice.

Name______________________________

Address______________________________

City ____________ State __________ Zip Code ________

Allow 4-6 weeks for delivery.
This offer is subject to withdrawal without notice.